# SHADOWS RISING

## A SHADOW CELL THRILLER

## ERNEST DEMPSEY

# 1

ISTANBUL

Adriana ducked her head a split second before the bullet thumped into the sedan's opposite quarter panel.

She cursed herself for being spotted. She'd spooked the target and now he was on the defensive, taking shots at her with a .45 cal, at least that's what it looked and sounded like.

Tracking down art that was stolen by the Nazis in World War II had its moments of peril, but those dangers had hardened her for what she was doing now: hunting terrorists.

The .45 fired again and shattered the window above her head. Whoever the driver was would certainly be less than happy when they got back to their vehicle and found it riddled with bullet holes and broken glass.

Pedestrians screamed as they scattered down the sidewalks and streets.

Despite today's shootout, Istanbul was a relatively peaceful city, only disturbed now and then by a bit of political unrest. Far and away, the ancient city formerly known as Constantinople was a bastion of multicultural enlightenment and acceptance. For thousands of years, the area was the crossroads between East and West. Wars had been fought to gain control of it. Conspiracies and secret alliances had been forged for this express purpose. Over time, rather than a military stronghold to be captured and utilized, Istanbul had become the center of much trade in that part of the world.

In the past, her expertise had been focused more intensely on art and the history surrounding it. After all, she was one of the most feared art thieves in the world. That fact didn't bother her. She only stole from people who'd come by their treasure through unscrupulous means. At the moment, Adriana didn't care about all the history and culture. She cared about not getting any of the citizens hurt, which was why she couldn't take a shot at the target despite the fact he was unloading a barrage from his magazine.

She wasn't in the business of taking out innocent civilians, but she needed to apprehend this guy or there would be trouble. Big trouble.

Adriana had been recruited by a secret counterterrorism organization known as Shadow Cell. Her friend June had been instrumental in bringing her on board, though it was witnessing a terrorist attack firsthand that drove Adriana to help. She had a life, a loving boyfriend, and a hobby that kept her busy enough. The family businesses and her trust fund kept her more than comfortable, giving her a life that many would envy.

Adriana Villa, however, wasn't one to sit on the sidelines and watch. She itched to be in the game.

So, here she was.

She'd tracked Qufar Abdi for nearly two weeks. The first intel she'd received about the terrorist was that he was in Greece, living on an island compound with a group of other terrorists connected to the Red Ring, an upstart cell that was spreading across the planet like a virus.

Shadow Cell operators had been able to confirm Abdi's location in Greece, but when Adriana arrived, he was gone. The compound had been abandoned, almost as if they knew she was coming, knew they were being watched.

Shadow Cell was too small and too tightly organized to have a mole. That meant someone got sloppy.

Adriana didn't assume anything. It could have been the director of the agency that messed up. All she knew was that her hunt for Abdi would likely get harder.

Luckily, she had been wrong.

Two days after striking out at the Grecian location, she got a lead from a source in Turkey.

Someone said they saw Abdi crossing the border with an entourage. Maybe they were bodyguards. Perhaps they were just more terrorist soldiers he recruited. Either way, it was better than nothing. Her vast network of lowlifes, degenerates, and scumbags was already proving its worth. Adriana wondered if the agency knew about her connections, and if so, whether they minded her using such sketchy assets. She had the feeling they wouldn't care so long as the job was done.

Now after casting a wide net, it seemed she'd caught the fish she was after.

Setting up surveillance was the most tedious part of the mission. Her orders were to follow Abdi, find out what he knew, who he was working for, and what the Red Ring was planning next.

As far as she knew, Abdi was a lower-level member of the terrorist cell. He wasn't brand-new, so he had some authority, but he certainly wasn't the one pulling the strings and issuing orders. Adriana knew if she played her cards right and was able to bring Abdi in for questioning, that would go a long way toward finding out who the mysterious head of the Red Ring really was and, perhaps, ending this whole debacle.

She had a feeling it wouldn't be that easy. Terror cells weren't like other entities. If you had a mad dictator trying to take over a region or a country, eliminating the leader often ended the conflict. It was the old adage that if you cut off the head of a snake, the body dies.

Terrorists, however, were different.

Cutting off one head simply meant that another would spring up somewhere else, eager to carry out their holy mission and perhaps be rewarded in either this life or the next.

Where other agencies and organizations failed to see that fatal flaw in their reasoning and planning, Shadow Cell went above and beyond. Not only would they track down and find the leader of the Red Ring, they would make him an example to anyone else in the world who considered terrorism as a viable option.

Adriana was driven by the people she'd seen dead or injured in the streets of Paris. She knew what men like Abdi and his cohorts were capable of. And she had no intention of letting anything like that happen again.

She'd cornered Abdi in a hotel room near the center of Istanbul. It was smart on his part to rent a place surrounded by so many people. He could easily blend in, and if things went south he could use millions of human shields to make his escape.

Another gunshot rang out above the screaming, and the bullet smashed into the wall behind her. Dust and debris exploded from the impact. He was getting less accurate. That meant he was trying to escape. A quick peek around the corner of the bumper confirmed her suspicion: Abdi was on the run.

Adriana knew that would be the case. She knew it from the second Abdi spotted her and realized who she was. Maybe he didn't know her name or who she worked for, but she'd slipped just enough to give away the fact that she was observing him, watching his every move.

He sprinted away through the flood of panicked pedestrians and disappeared into an alley.

Adriana sprang from her hiding place and charged ahead. Cars were parked on the street, their drivers choosing to take their chances on foot rather than stay put and be hit with a stray bullet. Adriana jumped as she reached an old beat-up sedan. She flew through the air, landing with her butt on the hood and sliding across the rest of the way until she felt her momentum and gravity bring her back to the asphalt.

Her eyes were locked straight ahead. She caught a glimpse of the target's shirt as he weaved through the mass of people in the alley's market. What had, a moment ago, been a place of business where farmers could hawk their wares, was now a funnel of chaos.

People rushed toward her as she pushed ahead. It felt futile, like she was swimming against a powerful rip current, but she kept going, grabbing shoulders, twisting her body, and pumping her legs. She could only hope Abdi had been slowed as much as she.

Finally, about forty feet into the side-street market, she broke through the last of the terrified citizens and tourists. She saw her target's foot disappear around a corner to the right.

*Gotcha.*

She rushed forward, but in an instant Abdi reappeared from around the corner with his pistol aimed right at her. He fired three times.

Adriana dove behind a column on the right and readied her weapon, holding it up by her face. The shooter's bullets tore into the evacuating crowd, striking two people—one in the leg and one in the back. The third round missed. Adriana assumed it had hit an exterior wall.

The two victims collapsed to the ground, rolling around and screaming. There was no way to be sure, but Adriana figured the wounds weren't mortal as long as they received medical attention soon.

The sirens echoing between the canyons of buildings told her help would be there soon.

The victims would be fine. She had a job to do, and now she was even more determined.

Driven by righteous anger, she popped out from around the column and aimed her weapon at the corner where Abdi had been just a moment before. There was no sign of him.

She sprinted from her cover and skidded to a halt at the corner. A quick peek around the corner revealed nothing but an empty street to the right that bent back to the left at a 90-degree angle.

Adriana took off again, but the gunman popped out again from around the next corner and opened fire. Bullets crashed into the corner, sending more red dust and debris into the air. She dove to her left and rolled until she reached the next wall, then pushed herself up and aimed her pistol.

Her finger tensed on the trigger, but she didn't fire. The target was gone again.

She cursed herself and got up once more. This time, though, she took a different tack.

He would run down the alley and find another place to hide, setting up his little ambush like he'd done twice already. She looked back and saw the street followed a similar pattern to the other, making a sort of forked path through the buildings.

She took a chance and rushed back the other direction.

Her feet pounded the cobblestone street; the clicking of her shoes reverberated through the three- and four-story apartments, cafes, and businesses. Vibrant fabrics were draped over the alley, keeping her in the shade for the most part but occasionally letting a streak of sunshine through.

Adriana came to another T-junction and looked both directions. She didn't need to think about it. The path to the right would take her toward Abdi and, hopefully, give her the element of surprise for a change.

She slowed her pace to an up-tempo jog in an attempt to be quieter as she hurried down the corridor toward the next corner. Halfway there, she stopped and pressed her back against the wall to her right and listened.

She heard something rustling just beyond her field of vision.

Abdi was finding cover.

She hadn't missed her guess.

Adriana tiptoed ahead, moving stealthily until she reached the edge of the building. She poked her head around for half a second and saw another alcove that connected to the alley.

And there he was. Abdi was waiting with gun in hand. He had his left shoulder pressed into the wall, ready to pop out and eliminate his pursuer at point-blank range. So, this was where he had decided to make a stand.

What he didn't realize is that by pigeonholing himself in the little dead-end side street, he'd sealed his fate.

She swung her left leg around the corner and pressed her heel into the stones. Then she crept forward, careful not to make a sound as she closed the gap between her and the target. She was out in the open and knew that any second he'd turn and see her or maybe catch a peripheral glimpse.

Adriana lined up the target in her weapon's sights, aiming for the shoulder that carried his gun. Her orders weren't to kill him. She was to bring him in for questioning.

One stray round could make her mission a moot point.

She had to be careful. While she didn't want to give the man a chance to surrender, she knew it was her best option. She also knew what would follow.

"Abdi!" she shouted. "Drop the weapon! I only want to—"

The gunman cut her off as she had expected. Startled, he twisted his body and turned the gun toward her. He never got off another shot.

She squeezed the trigger and planted a round straight through the tissue between his shoulder and neck. The bullet smashed into his collarbone, splintering it into fragments.

Abdi howled. The gun dropped from his hand and clattered on the cobblestone. He instinctively reached for the wound with his free hand, clutching it as he dropped to his knees in agony.

Adriana rushed forward and kicked his weapon out of reach, keeping her own trained on his head in case he decided to try something foolish.

But he was hurting too much to even consider making a break for it or trying to fight her off. He moaned like a baby.

"I told you I just wanted to talk," she said. "But you wanted to do it the hard way."

"You'll face your fate soon enough, American dog," he spat.

"Now, that's not any way to talk to a lady. I tried to extend an olive branch, and you just shove it in my face."

"You may as well kill me, infidel. You will get nothing from me."

She'd heard that before. Men who tried to keep secrets from her always confessed in the end, giving up everything they knew to save themselves from more pain. Over the years, she'd perfected the art of interrogation. It was how she'd been able to recover dozens of lost paintings and sculptures.

This guy, however, wasn't going to be the recipient of her talents. No, someone else wanted to speak with him.

She touched a button on her wireless earpiece. "I have the target," she said. "Requesting pickup."

"Ten-four," a female's voice came through the radio. "We have your location. Your ride will be there momentarily."

Adriana stared at the injured man. Blood seeped through the cracks between his fingers as he tried to stem the loss from his shoulder. He breathed heavily, like a man resigned to his fate. He didn't beg for mercy or to be released. Instead, he simply met her gaze with one of his own—a cold, calculating look that peered into her soul as if the look alone would convert her to his radical view of the world.

She wouldn't give in, though. Adriana was just as hardened as him, maybe more. Her emotions and will had been forged in the fire of the crucible more than once, and she'd come out stronger on the other side.

She heard an engine revving from down the street but never took her eyes off the coiled snake at her feet. She knew that, even injured, the man was dangerous and could snap at her in the blink of an eye.

The black sedan appeared around the corner and sped its way with almost no room on either side in the narrow street.

"Looks like your ride is here," she said and took a step back.

A man in a black suit got out of the front of the car. Another stepped out of the back. The trunk popped open, and the driver rushed around to prop it up.

One of the suits removed something from a jacket pocket—a syringe. He flicked off the plastic guard and bent down, shoving the needle into Abdi's arm. He depressed the pump and sent the drug into the man's bloodstream.

Within seconds, Abdi's eyelids grew heavy and he passed out.

"Good work, Agent Villa," the driver said as the other two men loaded the prisoner into the trunk. "Need a ride?"

"If you have room," she said with a smirk.

## 2

ISTANBUL-SHADOW CELL SAFEHOUSE

Adriana tossed her gear on a narrow hallway table made of oak and wrought iron. She tilted her neck to the left then right to stretch the muscles. One of the discs in her spine cracked, bringing a little relief to the tense tissue.

The agency's safe house was only fifteen minutes away—on the outskirts of the city—from where she'd apprehended Abdi. The men in suits had unloaded him from the trunk and brought him in the back through a red metal door.

Old warehouses were, apparently, easily rented for the right price.

Adriana wondered how many other properties Shadow Cell occupied throughout the world. She had a feeling it was on a need-to-know basis. The agency didn't strike her as the type to leave a big footprint. They were mobile, ready to zip across the globe at a moment's notice.

She let the thoughts go and wandered down the dusty hall. The drywall was cracked in several places. Wiring hung from an old light fixture above. One of the windows in a room to her right was broken, probably the result of some kid throwing rocks at the glass.

Down the hall, Adriana made a left and walked by a row of windows looking out into a courtyard. From the looks of it, the place used to be an epicenter of shipping and commerce. Now it was nothing more than a husk of its former self. Three tractor-trailers sat in loading docks, waiting for all eternity to receive their next shipment that would never come. The tires were flat, the edges scorched with dry rot.

She continued down the next hall until she reached another metal door. It was fixed with a plate in the center that protected a wire-reinforced window. She knocked twice, and the plate slid open. Sunglasses covered the eyes that looked out at her, despite the fact the guy was indoors.

The plate slid closed, and the door unlocked. It creaked open, and Adriana stepped inside the makeshift interrogation chamber. Once in, the guard closed and locked the door again.

"Hello, Addy," a familiar voice said from the corner.

Adriana didn't have to turn to see who it was. "Hello again, June. Good to see you." Then she turned and looked over her shoulder at her friend. "He was a feisty one." She pointed at Abdi.

"Yes, yes, he was. Shot two civilians in the process."

"I will shoot the both of you, too," Abdi said, looking up from the floor. His lip was bloody and swollen. Both eyes were black and equally enlarged from the rush of fluid flowing to the wounds and bruising. A long cut was oozing blood on his right cheek.

"Probably not, Qufar," June said, stepping away from the wall. "You don't know who you're talking to, do you?"

"American whores," he spat. A glop of blood and spittle hit the floor.

There were four men in suits in the room to watch over the prisoner. One of them stepped forward, about to backhand the guy for his rude comment, but June raised her hand and stopped him.

The guard stepped back to his position and folded his hands in front of his waist.

"You know that guys like you make it hard on the rest of the Middle Eastern population, right?" Adriana asked, addressing the prisoner.

He looked at her quizzically.

"Yeah. You think your little holy war is helping your cause, but in fact, more and more Muslims are getting sick and tired of your shenanigans. You're giving them a bad name, making it harder for them to travel and enjoy their lives, and honestly, they hate you for it."

He chuckled. "You think I care what you say? Do you think I care about the hordes of nonbelievers or those who sit on a fence, tolerating the poison dripping from the lips of the West? If I make their lives harder, good. They deserve no better. Allah himself should punish them."

June shook her head. "He's been like this since he got here. Won't listen to reason." She turned to the prisoner. "She's right, you know. Guys like you give Islam a bad name."

Adriana thought about one of her friends, a woman from Istanbul that had moved to the United States. They'd met in college. Last Adriana heard, she was living somewhere in the Southeast. She'd kick herself if it was Atlanta, but it had been years since the two connected. She remembered being at her friend's house when breaking news came across the television screen, showing scenes from the 9/11 attacks.

Adriana's friend had cursed loudly, letting slip a stream of profanity. There was no wondering why her friend was so angry. Adriana already knew. Acts of terror by extremists made life difficult for the rest of Islam. It would be weeks, maybe months, before her friend could even walk into a grocery store without being sized up by prying, paranoid eyes.

Men like Abdi were the cause of those problems. Not to mention the fact that they took the lives of innocent civilians all over the world without the slightest hint of remorse. That lack of guilt was splashed all over the prisoner's face, still visible through the layers of swelling, blood, and sweat.

June nodded to the side and made her way over to the corner of the room. Adriana followed to hear what her friend had to say.

When they were by a window, June looked out into the courtyard below. The sun bathed the facility in its warm embrace. Only a single cloud distorted the otherwise perfectly blue sky.

"He won't talk," June said.

"Looks like you worked him over pretty good."

"Didn't matter, almost like he enjoyed it."

Adriana turned her head and looked over her shoulder at the man bound to a chair.

"How far did you go?" Adriana asked.

June nodded in the guy's direction. "Just what you see."

Adriana nodded. "Leave me with him."

June's forehead wrinkled with concern. "Adriana, I don't think—"

"I'll be fine. Let me have ten minutes with him."

A sigh escaped June's lips, and she looked over at the prisoner. "Take as much time as you need. But I'm telling you, he's not going to talk."

"We'll see."

June motioned for the guards to follow her out of the room. When the door closed behind them, Adriana stalked over to her quarry and stood behind him for a long moment. She put her hand on his right shoulder and ran her finger, seductively, up his neck to his ear.

"So, what kinds of things did they ask you, Qufar?" She used his first name both to taunt him and to get his attention.

"I won't tell you anything. I am here on a mission from Allah. I answer only to him."

Adriana nodded. "I understand that." She tousled his hair and then stepped around in front of him. "Except that I'm pretty sure Allah won't appreciate you lusting after a woman."

His eyebrows furrowed. "What?"

She pulled her tank top down a little to show off her cleavage. He couldn't help but notice her skin, her pouting breasts, concealed by a thin layer of cotton. He shifted uneasily and averted his gaze to the wall in the far corner.

She lifted her leg and straddled his lap, lowering herself down slowly onto his thighs.

He moved again, trying to wiggle free, but it was no use. He was trapped.

Her scent wafted into his nostrils, filling him with the sultry smells of flowers and sandalwood. His heart pulsed quicker now no matter how much he tried to fight it. Adriana knew it would only be a matter of time until other things started getting aroused.

"Get off of me, devil woman," he said and spit in her face.

She fought off the disgust rising in her throat and wiped her cheek with the bottom of her shirt. In doing so, she revealed a section of her firm abdomen and a small patch of the black bra she was wearing under her top.

He swallowed hard and forced his eyes away again.

"How long has it been since you were with a woman, Qufar?" She leaned forward and whispered into his ear. "Too long?"

His breathing was quicker, full of desperation.

"I wonder if you've ever been with a woman."

"I...I have...long ago," he confessed. "But no more. I am a servant of Allah now. Nothing can change that."

She ran her fingers up the inside of his thigh. "I doubt that. And I doubt you've ever been with a woman like me."

"No. Please. I'm...I'm not permitted." He shifted and jolted like a bucking bull, but there was no getting her off him.

Adriana squeezed her legs tight against the outside of his. "Not permitted? Why is that?"

"To...gain admittance to...heaven, we must be pure."

"Oh, I see." She stroked the back of his head, her fingers getting tangled in the greasy black hair. He smelled like a homeless person who hadn't bathed in a month, but that didn't matter. She had him.

She reached down and unfastened the button on his pants.

"No, you can't do this," he said.

"No? Sure seems like I'm doing it."

"Please, stop."

"I'll stop...when I'm done."

"What do you want from me?" he demanded.

"I think you know," she said and let her finger drift down to the zipper.

"No, I can't."

"You can't—or you won't?"

"I'm not permitted," he repeated.

She leaned back, taking her hands off him, and removed her shirt. There was nothing between him and her but a thin black bra.

"Please," he begged.

"They beat you up, didn't they?" she asked. "They worked you over to find out what you know about the Red Ring."

"Yes."

"And what did you tell them?"

"Nothing. I told them nothing!"

"But you'll tell me."

"Never! I'll never tell a whore like you." The insult flew from his mouth with a mist of spittle.

She rolled her shoulders. "Very well." She reached back and unhooked the bra strap keeping the garment in place. The fabric sagged a little. "I'll just get what I want out of you and leave you to them."

"No, you can't."

"I am." She let the bra slip a little farther down, to the point where he could almost see everything. "And I'll tell you what else I'm going to do. I'm going to let you satisfy me while the cameras in the room film every second of it. Then we're going to send that footage to every known terrorist cell media outlet we know. My face will be blurred, of course, but yours...yours will be prominently displayed. I wonder how your bosses would feel about that. I'm guessing it would be frowned upon."

He swallowed hard again. Sweat rolled down his temples and dripped onto his shirt.

Adriana knew she'd hit the mark with her threat. This guy was trained to take as much physical pain as human beings could dole out. Sure, she'd thought about peeling off his fingernails or dislocating a few joints, maybe breaking some bones, but her comrades had already tried hurting him.

They hadn't tried appealing to his skewed sense of righteousness.

"I don't know his name, okay?" Abdi finally blurted out. "I've never met him. I'm just a lowly middleman. I get them what they want and leave it at a drop spot."

Adriana leaned back, placing her hands on his heaving chest. "Where?"

He breathed hard as if considering not telling her. A battle raged inside him, a war between the instinctual forces of his hormones and his beliefs. "Here, in Istanbul," he said, his voice full of regret. "It's a place here in Istanbul. I go there twice a week. Once to pick up a note with what they want listed on it. The second time is to drop off the goods."

"I need an exact location."

The words flowed quickly from his lips. When he was done telling her what she wanted to know, Adriana climbed off him and fastened her bra. She slipped her tank top back on, strutted over to the door, and flung it open.

"You get that?" she asked.

June was standing in the hallway with the guards. They'd heard the entire thing.

"Yeah," June said with a nod. "We got it."

"Good," Adriana said. "Don't tell Sean about that, okay?" Adriana had been dating Sean Wyatt for years now. He was often busy with his friend's International Archaeological Agency, traveling the world in search of ancient artifacts. The two occasionally found themselves in a heap of trouble. Sometimes that trouble involved Adriana. June was dating Sean's best friend, Tommy Schultz. It was fascinating how the four lives had come together in such an unlikely way. Yet here they were.

"Not a word," June agreed.

# 3

---

ISTANBUL

Adriana and June, with weapons ready, crouched behind a shipping container. The AR-15s weren't what Adriana was accustomed to using, but the weapon had proved itself in countless battles around the world and was now a first choice of aficionados back in the States. The two women had been monitoring the docks for the last four hours to make sure no one interfered with their stakeout.

The plan was simple. Wait for Abdi's connection to show up, send the whelp in to do the deal, and then catch the bigger fish.

Simple. Except in life, and especially this line of work, things were rarely that easy. If everything went according to plan, what a wonderful world it would be.

Adriana stole what was probably her five hundredth glance over at the cargo van parked in a corner lot where two concrete retaining walls met. The truck was old and beat-up to make it appear like it belonged in the abandoned docks—a derelict vehicle of yesteryear. In the back, she knew Abdi was being guarded by four agents with automatic weapons. If he so much as spit the wrong way, he'd pay dearly for it.

The prisoner had warmed to their plan, although Adriana and

June didn't fully trust he would stick to it. They'd promised him asylum—not in the United States but in Puerto Rico, where he could hide from his soon-to-be-former overseers for the rest of his life. He'd have a simple bungalow near the beach and a modest salary from the US government, but he'd be safe and wouldn't have to work again unless he wanted a more luxurious lifestyle.

Even with all that, Adriana had her doubts about the man. He was a snake, and she knew what snakes were capable of. They'd hide in the weeds, waiting for the opportune moment to strike when their prey least expected it.

"What's your status, Angel Two?" she said into the wireless radio connected to her ear.

"Bored, Angel One. What's it looking like out there?" The man's voice was gruff and sounded slightly irritated, probably at being given babysitting duty.

"All clear," Adriana said.

She peered around the giant steel box. The docks were situated on a little peninsula that jutted out into the Mediterranean. She could see why Abdi and his associates had chosen the location. The property hadn't been used in years, probably because more of the commercial shipping industry had moved to a different part of the city's coast. Based on the weathered For Sale signs hanging on the rickety fence surrounding the area, she figured few people came around other than the dregs of society looking for a place to sleep for the night in one of the abandoned warehouses or offices.

In America and in many other parts of the world, places like this were often the haven of drug addicts who'd lost almost any hope of returning to society.

So far, she hadn't seen any signs of such people, but she'd keep a lookout just in case. The last thing they needed was some whacked-out meth head stumbling into their ambush and spooking the targets.

There was still plenty of daylight left, but as the hours crawled by, Adriana started to wonder if Abdi's connections were going to show. She hadn't spent a lot of time doing these sorts of things. While there'd been dozens of missions where she'd had to wait on a mark, usually to get information out of them, running a clandestine operation against a serious terrorist threat was a different animal. Her previous line of work was more like a hobby, something she could walk away from whenever she felt like it. No one would get hurt. And the world would never be the wiser.

The stakes were much higher in this game. Astronomically so.

Adriana tucked back behind the container again and leaned her back against the warm metal.

June sensed her friend's impatience. "This sort of thing is a big part of what we do," she said. "Lot of sitting around and waiting. Sometimes, the bad guys don't even show up."

"What do you do when that happens?"

June smirked. "We hit the reset button, try to figure out what went wrong, and then set up another sting."

Sting was a funny term, at least Adriana thought so. It was a word cops used when they were taking down drug dealers or fences. She guessed it applied here, too, though she didn't like it. Then again, it didn't matter what it was called. The only thing that mattered was taking down the terrorists.

A motor groaned from around one of the buildings, and the two women perked up. They stood up and looked around the corners of the shipping container. Two black SUVs pulled around one of the abandoned buildings to the right, followed by a small moving van, not dissimilar to the one the prisoner was being held in.

As the vehicles stopped in the middle of a wide patch of asphalt between two cinder block buildings, men with submachine guns poured out of the SUVs and scattered. They took up defensive positions in pairs; setting up what was essentially a ring of death about a hundred feet across. The driver of the van got out when all the other men were in place and rushed around to the back to open the cargo bay door.

It was difficult to see what was inside, but Adriana figured it was empty since this was meant to be a pickup.

"Targets are in place," June said. "Time to put the pawn in play."

"Copy that, Angel One."

The cargo van inched forward, and a moment later Abdi climbed out. One of the guards motioned him to move forward to the cab.

The terrorist middleman looked scared. Adriana could see it in his eyes from fifty feet away.

She hoped he didn't flake out, or worse, do something stupid like run from them. Then they'd have to kill him. If that happened, there'd be a shootout, and from the looks of things her crew was slightly outnumbered. Even though the operators in the group were well-trained, covert ops guys that had been brought in from other agencies, she knew that guns were a great equalizer in a fight. Any idiot could get lucky with a bullet. It took a lot more skill to win a hand-to-hand fight.

Abdi made his way to the front of the truck and climbed in the passenger side. He'd been apprised of all the mission details, which included him riding in the front seat for the final leg. He knew the driver would be armed and ready to shoot him dead if he tried anything stupid. Adriana and June both knew that—if given the chance—people *would* do something stupid. So the driver was told to keep his weapon trained on the prisoner at all times during that stage of the operation.

"Package is on board," the driver said. "Moving into position."

The van pulled out of the corner and slowly drove into the thoroughfare. It passed the two women still crouching in their hiding spot and turned right, heading straight for the small army of men waiting in the middle of the landing.

The driver stopped the vehicle a dozen feet from the other van and put it in park. Abdi hopped out of the cab and looked around. The gunmen watching the center of the circle didn't move. Then the front passenger door of one of the SUVs opened, and a man in a white button-up shirt and black pants stepped out.

Adriana watched him carefully, doing her best to keep out of sight. The distance between her position and the targets was far enough that she'd be difficult to spot, but there were no guarantees. If one of the gunmen were to use binoculars or a scope, she'd stand out like an alligator at a crocodile party.

June kept one hand to her right ear. Unlike Adriana, she had two different earpieces. One was for communications; the other was for listening in on the conversation between Abdi and his associates.

One of the Shadow Cell operatives—Angel Three—was perched behind the retaining wall, hidden in some bushes and covered in camouflage with a long-range microphone. The device was delivering an isolated stream of sound from the arranged meeting. He was also equipped with an AR-15 with a long-range sniper scope in case things turned south.

"Khalil!" Abdi said with a tentative excitement. "I was starting to wonder if you guys were coming." Abdi had a nervous sound in his voice that June hoped he could squelch.

Maybe it was his natural way of speaking. Perhaps the others didn't notice.

"Why would you think that?" the man in the white shirt asked. His sunglasses glinted in the sun.

Abdi rolled his shoulders. "No reason. I've just been sitting here for a half hour. I was starting to wonder if I had the incorrect time."

"No," Khalil said. "You have the correct time. We were...held up momentarily." He turned and looked at the back of the truck. "The stuff in here?"

Abdi nodded and started to unfasten the lock on the back, knowing there were four men inside ready to apprehend the terrorist.

"Kind of a small vehicle for so many weapons, don't you think?"

Abdi frowned, distracted for a moment from his task. "I don't like to be wasteful. Why use a huge truck when a smaller one will do? I assure you: everything you asked for is in there."

Adriana learned that Khalil Tosu was an Albanian national with a nasty reputation. To call him a terrorist was a bit simplistic. He was much more than that. On top of being an extremist, he was also a businessman, profiting off the suffering of so many others.

June's dossier on the man explained that he'd grown up in one of the wealthiest families in Syria. Through a series of bad business deals with some unscrupulous Americans, his family had lost everything. They were cast into poverty, exiled from the people they once called friends.

Tosu learned the ways of the streets at a young age. He understood the code of eat or be eaten that the animals were so keenly aware of. So, he became something of an animal himself. He learned how to steal from those who had more than him.

By the age of thirteen, he'd killed a man. His victim had been just nineteen, but the fact that Tosu had managed to murder someone who was six years his senior filled the boy with a sinister confidence that swelled his ego to new heights.

Later on, as he grew into a fuller measure of treachery, he ran his organization like a Western drug cartel, using brutality and fear to keep rivals in line and to make sure his domain was secure. All along the way, he had exhibited an ironic religious fervor. He justified his actions by claiming he was the sword of Allah, the surgeon who had to cut out the *diseased* parts of the world to make it new again. Of course, Tosu was more than happy to profit off all that disease.

Apparently, selling slaves was also acceptable to Allah. A huge chunk of Tosu's empire was in human trafficking. Adriana had seen too much of that sort of thing going on in the last decade or so. Maybe it had always been there and she had been just too naïve to know about it.

Tosu had also become a prominent provider of weapons to certain extremist groups, including the Red Ring. As a result, he climbed the ladder of trust until he was fully integrated into their chain of command—if terror cells called it such a thing.

He and his men organized attacks on schools, churches, and other public places, at least that's what Shadow Cell's intel said. There was no way to verify that Tosu had a hand in those horrendous actions.

Adriana thought of Osama bin Laden, pinned for the World Trade Center and Pentagon attacks in 2001. She'd always wondered if he was the one truly responsible. The conspiracy theorist in her was always suspicious of the media and the lies they spun.

In the end, she figured bin Laden was probably guilty of something. This guy Tosu, however, was definitely guilty. Here he was, getting ready to transfer a truckload of what he believed were explosives and guns, weapons his men could use in the fight against the nonbelievers.

Abdi was fiddling with the lock. Adriana kept her eyes on him through a pair of binoculars.

"He looks nervous," she whispered.

"Affirmative," June replied. "Good thing he doesn't have to do the fighting."

Tosu put his hand on Abdi's shoulder and gently spun him around so the two men were standing face to face.

"What's he doing?" Adriana asked.

June didn't answer, simply shaking her head.

"Qufar, you have done well for our cause. You have provided us with weapons and supplies. We have struck a blow to the heart of the infidels thanks to your diligence." The man put his arm around Abdi's shoulder and started walking toward the waterfront. "That is why I wonder...."

Abdi cast a confused, sidelong glance at Tosu. "Wonder what?"

The two strolled to the edge of the harbor where concrete and asphalt met the sea.

Tosu turned and faced his supplier. "I wonder why you would help the Americans and British."

Abdi's face filled with confusion. "What? What are you talking about?"

"Oh no," June said. "They're onto us."

# 4

ISTANBUL

"What?" Adriana asked.

Tosu pulled a pistol out of his waistband and held it at his side, tilting the barrel at the bewildered Abdi.

"You think we don't know what you've been doing, Qufar?" Tosu asked. "We planned this whole thing."

"What? What do you mean?"

"We knew you were being followed. We know they're listening right now, watching. I have to say, while I'm disappointed by your treachery, you have done well in leading them into our trap. So, in a way, I suppose I should be thanking you."

Abdi swallowed hard. His lips quivered.

"Thank you," Tosu said. The pistol's muzzle flashed. The pop echoed through the wharf.

A pink mist exploded from the back of Abdi's skull. His body wavered for three long seconds and then toppled into the water with a splash.

"No!" June said and popped out from her hiding place.

Another gunshot rang out from near the truck. One of Tosu's gunmen was holding a pistol in the air, pointing it at a newly shattered window. The driver slumped over out of sight.

The gunman climbed in the cab, started the vehicle, and shifted it into gear.

"Angel Two, open the cargo door and get out of there. They know!"

"Copy that," the man's voice came through the radio.

The van was already rumbling toward the sea where Tosu stood.

"Angel One," the man said through the radio, "the door is locked from the outside. It won't budge."

"Dear Lord," June said. "Angel Three—"

"I'm on it," another voice said.

The guy behind the retaining wall took aim at the truck's cab, but he couldn't get a clean shot at the driver. So he turned the barrel slightly and squeezed the trigger.

One of Tosu's gunmen dropped to the ground, the back of his skull now a bloody canoe.

The man next to him turned to face the threat, but he caught a round in the base of his neck and dropped to the pavement.

"Take out the truck's tires!" June said in a tone that was nearly a shout.

The sniper turned the barrel again and lined up the crosshairs of his scope with the van's back-left tires. He fired. The bullet pinged off the hard ground. He shot again and again, faster this time, now fully aware of what was at stake. The driver jumped out of the cab at the last second as one of Angel Three's rounds struck a tire. The van dipped on the back-left corner but kept rolling toward the waterfront. He squeezed the trigger repeatedly, trying to get a clean look at the front-left tire. If he could hit it, the van would likely lurch to the left and circle back to safety.

He stopped firing for a second to calm himself, then aligned the crosshairs with the front of the vehicle, waiting for the tire to come into view. The van wobbled to the left. Angel Three let out a long breath, steadied his nerves, and fired.

The round zipped through the air at lightning speed. He thought for sure he'd hit the mark.

Unfortunately, the truck hit a bump and swung slightly to the right a split second after the sniper fired.

"Crap," he said into the radio.

Adriana and June watched as the van hit the chain barricade separating the water from land. The truck only paused for a second before it broke through the chain and the heavy posts moored to the pavement. The vehicle groaned and tipped forward, gravity sucking the engine down to a watery grave, the hood crashing into the water. The van bobbed for a moment before it started a nosedive to the bottom of the sea, slowly sinking a few inches at a time as it filled with water.

"No!" June shouted as she spun around from her hiding place.

She whipped her weapon around, took aim at one of the gunmen, and fired. The round hit him in the abdomen and dropped him to his knees.

Angel Three's actions had already drawn the attention of Tosu's men. They'd ducked for cover wherever they could find it and were now poking their heads out to try to find the shooter. When they saw June stalking toward them with weapon blazing, they clambered out from behind cover and opened fire.

Adriana knew her friend was acting hastily despite her extraordinary training. Emotions had no place in a gunfight. They could get you killed. So, Adriana stepped out from behind the steel box and searched for a target.

Angel Three's weapon fired again, the report booming over the docks like thunder. One of the shooters fell on his back. Adriana aimed at the guy next to him and squeezed the trigger even as she moved forward. She kept on the balls of her feet so the weapon in her hands would stay steady.

Her gun fired one round at a time. She knew she'd be more accurate with semi automatic shots as opposed to full auto. Another gunman fell to her weapon, this one taking a bullet to the forehead.

June continued her rampage, emptying her magazine at a cluster of four gunmen crouching behind a stack of pallets.

"Backup, move in," Angel Three said into the radio. "Go! Go! Go!"

He wasn't the one in charge of the mission, but he took the initiative after June left her position to lead the attack.

Four more operatives who'd been covering the gate by the street sprang into action. They rushed down the short hill and into the fray, fanning out as they moved forward.

The second they were in range, the men opened fire. The cacophony of guns made the wharf sound like an urban war zone. One of the reinforcements took a bullet to the thigh and dropped to one knee with a yelp. That didn't stop him from continuing his assault from there. He continued firing on the terrorists' position to his left, bombarding them with a deadly hail of metal.

June and Adriana kept moving forward like two immortals, unafraid of the death whizzing by them.

One by one, the terrorists fell until there were only two remaining, hiding behind another shipping container next to a storage building.

Adriana saw a sudden movement behind one of the SUVs. A flash of white behind the hood told her Tosu was on the run.

She fired a round at the vehicle, but one of the last gunmen popped out of his hiding place and took a shot at her. She dove out of the way and returned fire, planting a bullet in his shoulder. The force of the round spun him around for a second before one of the reinforcements took him down with a flurry of shots.

Adriana sprang to her feet and charged forward. The SUV with Tosu inside squealed its tires and sped away in a cloud of white smoke. Adriana didn't care about the target getting away right now. She had to save the men in the truck.

Her feet pounded the pavement faster and faster until she'd reached the edge of the docks. The back of the van was about one foot away from being completely submerged. She stuffed her weapon in her belt even as the men behind her finished killing off the last of Tosu's men. Without hesitation, she jumped over the edge and landed on the big van door.

She could hear the men inside pounding on the door, screaming for help. She knew the water would almost be at the top and their narrow patch of air would soon be gone.

A muffled bang from inside was followed immediately by a hole exploding through the door. The men inside were trying to shoot their way out. Their desperation had reached its zenith.

She rapped hard on the door. "Hey! Friendly fire! I'm gonna get you guys out!"

The van shuddered. It sank another six inches almost instantly. Adriana lost her balance for a second. She bent her knees and crouched down, planting her palm against the back of the door. It was all she could do to hope none of the men inside would fire again.

"Help us!" one of the guys screamed.

Adriana knew in a few seconds the screaming would stop. The eerie silence would signal the water had covered their faces. When that happened, they'd have a minute, maybe two depending on how long each guy could hold his breath.

She worked her way over to the lock and wiggled it. Abdi's key was gone. She'd seen him put it in the keyhole, but now there was no sign of it. *Only one thing left to do,* she thought.

She raised her weapon and pointed it at the lock, holding it less than a foot away. Her finger tensed on the trigger, and then the truck surged down again. Water rushed over the back of the van and covered her feet. It was sinking faster now, set on a course for the bottom of the sea that would drown the men inside. In less than ten seconds, the water was up to her knees and rising rapidly.

Adriana slid over to the lock and ducked her head under the water. She found the object and shoved the muzzle up against it. *This would be close,* she thought. Shooting the lock underwater would require it to be pressed directly up against her weapon since bullets lost a ton of momentum once they hit liquid. Keeping the muzzle flush with the lock would prevent that, but it could also blow off her fingers. Then there was always the chance shrapnel from the blast would damage the nerves in her hand.

Those concerns flashed through her head in the briefest of

moments. They didn't matter. The only thing that mattered was saving the men inside the van.

She raised her head, took a breath, then ducked back under the surface and spied the lock one last time. Her finger tensed on the trigger and fired.

The recoil under the sea was much less than in the air above, but the gun did its job. The bullet tore through the tough metal exterior and freed the mechanism within. Adriana yanked the lock from the housing and slid the door handle free. Then, as the warm Mediterranean water rose to her shoulders, she grabbed the bottom rung of the door and pulled as hard as she could.

# 5

ISTANBUL

Adriana leaned against one of the steel shipping containers as the sun dipped toward the horizon to the west. Her clothes were soaked. Thankfully, she wasn't cold.

The men she'd saved from a watery grave were clustered on the ground behind an ambulance. None of them were seriously injured, so the presence of the emergency vehicle and paramedics was a mere formality, a precaution June took to make sure they were all right.

June strolled over to where Adriana was standing. She placed her shoulder on the Spaniard's shoulder. "You saved those guys' lives."

There were no more accolades, no more praise. The one sentence, June felt, was enough.

Adriana gave an absentminded nod. "I couldn't save the driver."

June shook her head and looked out toward the setting sun. "No. None of us could." Regret filled her voice. "I should have seen this coming."

"Don't blame yourself. There's no way we could have known."

June didn't buy it. "No. I pride myself on covering every possible angle, every potential threat. It never occurred to me that Abdi wanted to be caught so he could lead us here."

"Are you sure that's what happened?"

June rolled her shoulders. "Sure seems like it."

"I doubt he would have done that if he'd known Tosu was going to kill him."

"True. Unless he didn't think Tosu would do that."

Adriana sighed and followed her friend's gaze out to the glistening blue sea. "I could hear genuine fear in Abdi's voice. I don't believe he was trying to get caught; however, his getting apprehended could have been part of Tosu's plan."

June gave a nod. "You're probably right. Abdi *did* sound afraid, like he didn't know what was going to happen. Tosu, on the other hand, must have known what was going on. Abdi was under surveillance during his entire stint with us. He had no way to communicate with the outside world. That means Tosu set this whole thing up to get to us."

"You think he knows who we are, what Shadow Cell does?"

"Hard to say," June answered with a shrug. "There's no way to know. I doubt he has information on our identities, headquarters, and that stuff. If anything, he probably thinks CIA or another agency is hunting them down. He knows about the hunt but not the hunter. In that regard, we still have the advantage."

"But in the other regard?" Adriana let the question hang.

"We lost our primary lead. Tosu escaped. Abdi is dead. And we are starting from square one."

It was a heavy blow to their operation. Had they been able to apprehend Tosu, they might have been able to extract information from him about the scope of the Red Ring.

Then again, a man like him may have gone to his grave without giving up even a crumb of helpful intel. Difficult to say.

They'd banked on taking him down and using him to learn as much as possible about the Red Ring. Maybe they'd invested too much hope in him. Adriana felt like that's exactly what Shadow Cell had done in their pursuit of Tosu.

The worst part of failing was the immediate threat he posed to innocent people. Who knew where he would strike next?

At least he hadn't gotten the weapons he wanted.

That last thought loomed in Adriana's mind.

"It was definitely a setup," she said after a few seconds spent processing the events. "He knew there were no weapons. He knew there'd be men inside the truck, or at the very least he assumed there would be."

"Yeah," June said.

"He killed off one of his primary suppliers. That means he'll be in the market for another one." There was a twinge of hope in her voice.

"True, but we have no way to find him. He's a ghost, Adriana. Abdi was our only link to him. The guy will vanish again. And this time, he won't resurface."

Adriana wasn't so sure. "Where do all these guys go to find guns, bullets, explosives?"

"Usually, they have a series of connections, people in the black market they know. I'd say trust, too, but it's a slippery slope to trust anyone in the arms underworld."

"Right. Where else could they go for those things?"

"I suppose they could shop on the dark web, but federal agencies monitor that pretty diligently."

Adriana thought of some of the horrific things she'd heard about on the dark web. Recipes for cooking human meat; young children for sale; and a plethora of other sickening things. It was the ultimate den of online iniquity, a place for the blackest of souls to hawk their wares and ply their trade.

With all that repulsive stuff happening on the dark web, she wondered why these agencies June referred to didn't step in and take action. The answer that immediately popped into her head was even more nauseating than the things she'd heard about the digital underworld: they—the clandestine government agencies—were allowing it to happen. Maybe June didn't know as much about her peers as she thought.

That was another rabbit hole to chase at another time. For now, Adriana focused on the thing her friend mentioned before.

"Who do you know in the black market that could help us?"

June scratched her head and thought. She didn't answer immediately. "My connections," she said finally, "are limited in the criminal underworld. What about your friend? You think he might be able to help us?"

Adriana knew who she meant. The guy who called himself A-Tak —real name Raymond—had helped them before, but it was anyone's guess if he would do it again.

She already owed him one favor. She doubted there was any way to get around him asking for compensation this time. Of course, she could always play the law-dog card now. Maybe. Threatening someone who'd helped her in the past didn't seem like a good way of doing business. Perhaps there was another way to enlist his help.

"I'd hardly call Ray a friend," Adriana said. "But I suppose, considering the circumstances, he's the closest thing to a friend we might have. I'll give him a call and see what he's up to. If I had to guess, he's probably knee deep in vodka and gambling debts."

"Model citizen."

Adriana shrugged. "Everyone has their vices. Although Ray definitely has a knack for finding trouble."

"Maybe we need someone like that right now," June said. "We've done a pretty good job of finding trouble ourselves. Sounds to me like he'll be in good company."

Adriana nodded. "I'll see what I can do."

She watched as June wandered back over to where the other operators were sitting around on the ground next to the ambulance. The men were shaken, but they'd endured worse—maybe not worse scares than drowning, but they'd faced death before. Adriana knew that one or two of them were Navy SEALs. The others had also gone through incredibly difficult training to get into the spec ops of their respective military branches.

She'd seen one of the toughest parts of SEAL training in a video a few years ago. It involved submerging the recruits in ice-cold water repeatedly. She didn't recall all the details but imagined it was nearly impossible to get through it—both mentally and physically.

June checked on the men, talking briefly to each one as she hovered over them.

Adriana knew June was a good person. She was kind and caring but also capable of dealing out swift and merciless justice to those who needed it.

Her bravado at the docks could have gotten her killed. Adriana considered chatting with her friend about that, about keeping emotions pushed aside and being more precise, more careful. Then she thought better of it. Now wasn't the time. Emotions were still high. Maybe they could discuss it later.

Adriana turned away and trudged up the hill, leaving June and the authorities at the wharf to finish whatever cover-up they were going to implement. It was a wonder to Adriana how so many people could be blinded by the simplest of lies. The cops, emergency crews, everyone down there except her team would be told some kind of tall tale that they would invariably accept as truth.

So it was, living in the shadows.

Now, it seemed, she was about to dive deeper into the darkness once more. She fished out her phone and looked at the screen. Luckily, this newest version was waterproof. She pulled up her list of contacts as she rounded the corner at the top of the hill and headed down the sidewalk toward her car.

Ray wouldn't answer her call, so she stared at the number for a moment before sliding the phone back in her pocket.

*Into the shadows again*, she thought.

# 6

DULIN

DUBLIN

T he door opened with a creak. The old Bow Street distillery, where one of Ireland's most famous whiskeys was once produced, had been converted into lofts and single-family apartments. With the new construction, Adriana found it odd that the hinges made such a squeaky sound.

She'd cursed both the tenant and the landlord for not slapping some WD-40 on the hinges, or at the very least a little oil.

So much for a quiet entry.

She swung the door shut as fast as possible to minimize the sound and slowed its momentum just before it hit the frame. She twisted the doorknob and then gently released it so the bar would slide quietly into the receiver.

Adriana scanned the room as she always did when entering a strange place. She'd never been to Ray's new apartment. In fact, tracking him down had been something of a chore. It took two days before she could locate him.

Ray, or A-Tak as he was known in the hacker community, was incredibly careful about hiding his online footprint, and for good reason. He'd committed internet crimes in nearly every European country and was wanted in several of them, at least for questioning.

Adriana knew the deeds Ray performed were essentially harmless to the population at large. He didn't steal money from people's bank accounts. Identity theft wasn't his thing—unless it was someone who'd screwed over good, hardworking people.

He'd been a sort of *hacktivist* for several years now; handpicking his targets from a short list of society's worst and wealthiest. He was no digital Robin Hood, although he often contributed to charity. He took only what he needed, spread the wealth with others who needed it more, and then used whatever he could find against the target— usually uncovering a scandal of some kind.

While Adriana wasn't sure how she felt about his flexible morals, she did have a deep respect for Ray. She'd downplayed June's calling him Adriana's friend, but the truth was, in this world she was about as close to a friend as Ray probably had.

He spent so much of his life in the dark, entrenched in the digital world of code and pixels, there wasn't much time for socializing.

On her end, she figured it was probably best to keep a safe distance. Guys like him pushed the envelope. They tested waters that —eventually—would be full of sharks looking for a meal. Sooner or later, he'd piss off the wrong person, or group, and they would come after him.

He was careful. Adriana would give him that. But even the most cautious hunter could eventually become the hunted.

She noted three high-definition computer monitors in the back-right corner near a window. One of them displayed an ordinary desktop. The other two were full of code that continued scrolling up at a steady pace. The machines cast an eerie glow into that part of the room. There was a jacket on an orange couch, but other than that, the place was remarkably clean for a hermit like Ray.

Adriana figured there would be empty pizza boxes or beer bottles lying around everywhere.

"I didn't think you were going to bother me anymore," a familiar voice said. It came from the shadows of a doorway to the left.

Adriana didn't answer. His sudden comment startled her, but she didn't let it show. Some people would have jumped out of their shoes. Not her. She'd gotten over that nervous tendency years ago.

"I suppose you need my help with something," Ray said, stepping from the doorway. The light of the monitors struck him and revealed a gun in his hand, held waist high.

"This how you treat all your guests?"

His head turned once to the right. "I don't have guests. And you weren't invited."

"I never am." She kept her voice cool and even, almost seductive in a weird sort of way.

He swallowed. "What do you want, Addy?"

"You already said it. I need your help."

He bit his tongue for a second. He winced dramatically, showing her he was frustrated. Then he stepped over to the counter and put the gun on the surface.

"You're lucky I didn't kill you."

"Is that thing even loaded?"

"Yes." His voice was unsteady. "Okay, no. You have any idea how hard it is to get bullets around here?"

"I'm surprised it's a real gun."

He snorted. "Pfft. It's real."

"Hardly a useful tool without the things that make it go bang-bang." Her wry smile melted his defenses.

He turned and strolled over to the corner where his machines were downloading and uploading information. He leaned over the desk, checking something on one of the monitors, and then stood up straight again.

Adriana took a few steps deeper into the apartment. "What is all that?" she asked. "Downloading pirated movies?"

"Ha. I'd tell you what I'm doing, but then I'd have to kill you."

She rolled her eyes at the clichéd joke. "Kill me with what? Your gun that has no bullets?"

"Did you come here just to give me grief, or do you really need my help? What are you doing in Dublin, anyway? I moved here because of you, by the way."

He wandered back into the kitchen and grabbed a beer out of the fridge. He popped open the bottle and took a swig. Most of the drinkers his age would be at one of the Dublin pubs like the Stag's Head or Temple Bar. Ray was an introvert. That was putting it mildly.

She noted an empty grocery box next to the door. It had probably been delivered the previous day. She imagined he did most of his shopping online simply to avoid contact with other people.

"No, I didn't come here to give you grief," she said. "That's just an added bonus." She curled her lips in a way that shut down any irritation.

He took another sip of beer and set the bottle on the counter. "I'd ask how you found me, but I don't think I want to know."

"Or maybe you already do."

He snorted. "Yeah, I probably do. One of my connections squealed, didn't they? Who was it? Gil? I bet you didn't have to do much to get him to talk."

"It wasn't Gil. And it doesn't matter. I've already spent two days trying to track you down, so if you don't mind, I'd like to get to it."

He put his hands out wide, wondering what she was waiting for.

"We've been tracking another terrorist," she said.

His head turned to the side in dramatic fashion, like he couldn't believe what he was hearing. "Oh no. Not this again. Tell me you're not still chasing terrorists."

"I am. And just like before, if you let that secret out, I really will have to kill you. And the bullets in my gun are very real."

She opened her leather jacket just enough for him to see the weapon inside hanging from her shoulder.

He tried to read her expression to tell if she was joking or not. There wasn't a crack on her face that indicated she was.

"You...wouldn't really. Would you?" he asked, a little disconcerted.

"Probably not." She let the jacket fall back to its place. "But I would beat the crap out of you."

"Fair enough," he said with a goofy nod. Then he strode past her and slid into the rolling chair at his workstation. He spun around to face her and crossed one leg over the other. "All righty then, who are we looking for?"

Adriana reached into the other side of her jacket and produced a folded piece of paper. She moved across the room with what Sean had called deadly grace and handed the paper to Ray.

"This is Khalil Tosu," she said. "I need to find him."

"Obviously. You kind of already said that." Ray looked over the paragraph of information next to the black-and-white image of Tosu. "Known arms dealer. Fundamentalist. Killer. Sounds like this guy is a Grade A piece of crap."

"Indeed. My team and I were in the middle of apprehending him when the operation took a turn. Tosu got away. One of our men was killed in the process, although we took out over a dozen of his goons." She ticked her head up. "You ever heard of him?"

He stared at the picture and then finally shook his head. "I...I don't think so."

"You don't sound certain."

"I'm not. I mean, there are lots of guys like this out there. Usually, I try to steer clear of these types. You know me; I like to avoid trouble."

That much she did know. It was one of the reasons hackers like him went with nicknames or some kind of alias.

"But this guy," he went on, "there's something familiar about him. I can't put my finger on it. Seems like I've seen him somewhere before, but I'm not sure."

"Here in Dublin?"

"No," he shook his head slowly and handed the paper back to her. "No, I don't think so. I haven't been here that long, and the few times I've gone out I didn't really make eye contact with many people."

"Sounds like you live a lonely life." She let her lips crease on the right corner.

He guffawed. "Please. Loneliness is a state of mind. I have needs, sure, but that's easily taken care of. I don't have time for relationships. Would slow me down too much."

"I feel like we've had this conversation."

"Yeah. So anyway, I can throw out a net and see what comes back. Some of my buddies in London might have some info on this dude. It may take a while, though. How fast you need to find him?"

She gave a stern look that told him everything he needed to know.

"That soon, huh? This guy must be a problem."

"You read that summary. When we lost him, he was in the middle of a deal to get weapons to one of his terror cells. We don't know where the shipment was going, only that he was the pickup guy orchestrating everything. He knew we were there, knew we were setting a trap for him. We were lucky to get out alive."

"Sounds like you got yourself a mole," he said, sticking his finger out for a second.

"We have people working on that issue. My job is to find Tosu and bring him in."

"Okay. I'll help you. For my usual fee, of course."

"How about I don't remove your kneecaps as a down payment?"

He pouted his lips and nodded. "Yeah, that works."

Then he spun around and started typing on the keyboard. She watched as he entered lines of code, his fingers flying across the keys in a flurry of rapid taps. Adriana was pretty fast with her typing skills, but she'd never seen someone capable of Ray's speed.

He stopped for a second and stared at the center screen, then spun around and crossed his arms.

"What?" she asked. "There a problem?"

"Yep," he said. "You know the rules."

She let out a long sigh. "Are you serious with this?"

He answered with an exaggerated nod.

She took a deep breath and exhaled. "Fine. A-Tak, will you please help me find this terrorist?"

He displayed a wide, silly-looking grin. "See? Was that so hard? Now I can help you."

Ray spun back around and started working again. "You can sleep on the couch as long as you need," he said without looking back at her. "Might be nice to have a guard dog around for a day or so."

She rolled her eyes for the second time and pulled up a chair to watch him work. Adriana lingered a few feet back, not wanting to make him uncomfortable or cramp his workspace.

Ray worked at the computer for over an hour without getting up to so much as use the bathroom. The only time he paused was to ask Adriana to grab his beer off the counter in the kitchen. Other than that, he was more focused than anyone she'd ever seen. The only people even close were the kids back in Tommy's lab in Atlanta. They were the same kind of geniuses as Ray: introverted, a little quirky, and preternaturally smart.

Adriana's eyes were growing heavy by the time Ray finished setting up his online net. He let out an exhausted sigh and leaned back in the chair. Then he stretched his arms up high and linked his fingers, pressed the hands against the back of his skull, and craned his neck until the vertebrae let out a relieving crack.

"I think that's got it," he said.

She yawned and covered her mouth. "That will find Tosu?"

"Based on what you told me, this guy is still looking for weapons. Your little operation might have been torpedoed, but that doesn't mean he's not still shopping. All we have to do is wait until he makes a mistake."

"And if he doesn't?"

"Well, then you're up a creek without a paddle."

She frowned at the expression. She'd spent a ton of time in the United States, especially in recent years, but that phrase was one she'd not heard before.

It was Ray's turn to roll his eyes. "It means you're screwed."

# 7

TIRANA, ALBANIA

The phone in Tosu's smoking room rang. The shrillness of the noise and its loud volume startled him briefly. Khalil Tosu wasn't a man given to being surprised often. Those who tried typically ended up with a bullet in their skull, even if the surprise had been a good one.

He didn't take chances. It was how he'd survived so long in such a dangerous world.

Growing up in Yugoslavia, he'd been raised in a poor home. Communism was failing. And for practicing Muslims like his family, they lived under a constant threat of being taken in the middle of the night and driven to some far-off place to be executed.

When the regime collapsed and war ensued, Tosu had been a young man of nineteen. The fighting was fierce between the warring factions, and in the end new countries were forged from the chaos and spilled blood.

His parents had been killed when an American bomb struck their apartment building. Probably an accident. Or maybe there had been a high-priority target somewhere nearby. Either way, the deaths of his parents only served to push him further from any semblance of tolerance toward the United States and the countries it helped.

Out of the destruction, Tosu formed his own little empire, sneaking weapons to anyone willing to kill Americans or their allies. He started simple at first, organizing raids that did little more than piss off the enemy. As time went on, he became more adept at organization, strategy, and taking command rather than trying to carry out his own orders.

When the Red Ring found him, it was nothing more than a fledgling organization looking to strike back at the nonbelievers around the world. With his vision, he'd helped it grow to so much more.

Drunken revelers had been killed in nightclubs around the globe. One of his men had struck a gay bar in the United States, executing more than thirty people and injuring fifty before the police interfered and cut him down in a hailstorm of bullets.

Tosu was proud of the soldier. He'd been a warrior for Allah and struck at the heart of the West's putrid tolerance of radical abominations. Their leader had applauded both the soldier's sacrifice and the ability of Tosu to get the man into place to strike with the biggest impact.

There were other attacks of course: Paris, London, Brussels, and Amsterdam, just to name a few. Tosu had been the mastermind behind all of them, pulling the strings for each blow the Red Ring struck against the infidels.

Of course, his men almost always died in the attacks. With promises of eternal glory and their every fantasy provided by the Almighty, they had very few reservations about taking on suicide missions. Their sacrifice, Tosu knew, would continue to escalate growing awareness of the sins of the nonbelievers. Through their martyrdom, a new kingdom would rise, one that was free of the disgusting practices of the West, one of purity and righteousness.

Well, maybe a little of those things. Tosu was no saint. He fed his carnal urges like any man. The money he made from his various activities provided a legion of women at his beck and call. And none would dare deny him.

He justified his sins by reminding himself, and perhaps even his maker, that he was doing Allah's work in bringing the infidels to their knees. Why shouldn't he have a little reward for his efforts? After all, if they were going to be given dozens of virgins upon arriving in paradise, why shouldn't he have a few of those same delights in this life?

Tosu looked over at the phone and waited for a moment to make sure it was going to ring again. He knew only a handful of people had that number, so odds were it was an important call. Even so, he wasn't going to get up unless he was certain.

He took another draw on his cigar as the phone rang. Shafir wouldn't appreciate being forced to wait.

The smoke spiraled upward in a blueish-gray stream. Then he blew it away with a burst from his lips and stood up.

After the failed ambush in Istanbul, he'd managed to escape with his driver to their rendezvous point, a small safe house apartment in the heart of the city. He'd underestimated the strength of his enemies and their abilities. Most of his men died there on the docks that day. He knew their sacrifice would come with great reward, but that did little to wipe away the anger boiling in his heart. He thirsted for revenge, and the faces of the two women who led the charge burned in his mind.

Who dared interfere with their plans? It was the second time someone had gotten in the way. The previous time—an intricately planned missile attack on a soccer stadium—would have been as big if not bigger than the September 11 attack on the World Trade Center and the Pentagon. Estimated casualties would have been tenfold.

Of course, the governments of the West would have rallied their forces and pushed out to attack someone, just as they'd done in 2001. It was what the public wanted, after all. The mindset of Americans, especially, was more focused on getting their brand of justice than actually figuring out who was responsible.

They'd pinned the attacks on Osama bin Laden, but it was anyone's guess who was really responsible.

Tosu had a few ideas, but he'd never shared them with anyone. It honestly didn't matter. The fact was, the attack was a huge success, and now the countries full of nonbelievers were looking over their shoulders every time they walked into a grocery store, a movie theater, or even a hospital. No one felt safe anymore. The only way they'd ever feel that way again was through death or conversion. Tosu was happy to give them the former.

The number on the phone display was one he recognized and one he didn't want to receive. But he couldn't ignore it. The man on the other end of the line would accept such treatment as an act of treachery.

While Tosu was one of the most powerful men in the Red Ring, he still had people to answer to. One of them was the guy calling him at that moment.

"Hello," he said in a cool tone.

"What happened?" a gruff, heavily accented voice said.

Tosu knew what the call would be about. The leader wanted answers. That was a given. Tosu would desire the same thing were their positions reversed. In fact, he was curious as to how the enemy was able to react as quickly as they had.

"The ambush went according to plan."

"Really?" Shafir asked. "Because last I checked, you lost several men. More than ten, I believe. And the ones responsible managed to get away."

"Yes, that is unfortunate, both losing men and the infidels escaping. But I assure you, they won't bother us again."

There was a pause on the other end of the line. "How can you be so certain? If they have beaten us once, they can do it again. And next time could be worse."

Tosu didn't have to ask what the man meant by that. He knew that being captured was worse than being killed. The Americans and the British were renowned for their unethical means of getting prisoners to talk.

On the outside, their agencies preached the Geneva Convention and fair treatment to those captured in times of war and otherwise. On the inside, however, they used any and all methods to get what they wanted. It was one of the best-kept secrets on the planet.

While the variations were different, there was always the same thread that ran through their interrogations: There would be an escape attempt story that ended with the prisoner being shot dead, or something along those lines. The claim would be self-defense and that the shooters didn't have a choice, but Tosu knew better. It was one of the reasons his soldiers fought to the death rather than face torture at the hands of the nonbelievers.

Now and then, there would be an accident story that barely made the back pages of the news. It could be a prison bus crash that killed several key inmates, or possibly even a "suicide" in a cell. The thoughts enraged Tosu, but he tempered his emotions and stuck to the topic at hand.

"We are tracking their movements as we speak, great Teacher," Tosu said. It was a lie, but one he knew Shafir would buy.

The truth was Tosu didn't have a clue where the two women or their cohorts were. It was evident that they were working for some kind of extrajudicial agency. Only a well-funded, well-managed organization could equip soldiers with that kind of training and those types of weapons. The way the women moved had been too precise for it to be some kind of organized crime syndicate set on robbing him and his men of a big weapons haul.

No, they were working for someone, but who? CIA? Some other branch of special ops? They were such a nuisance, always playing world police, sticking their noses in places they shouldn't be. Tosu knew he'd have to wait for the answer, but he had a plan to get it.

"If you're tracking them, why not kill them now and be done with it?"

Great. The Teacher saw through the lie. Or did he? It was, after all, a logical question.

"A wise man once told me that to kill the beast, you don't cut off its arms or legs; you cut off the head." Tosu hoped quoting his master would temporarily sate the man's thirst for answers.

"Your flattery is appreciated, but that still doesn't answer my question."

"We can kill their agents, great Teacher. We can eliminate them by the dozens, but that won't stop them from coming. They will descend upon us like a flood, greater and greater until we are over-whelmed. We need to find out where they're coming from, who is pulling the strings to these puppets."

The leader fell silent for a moment, considering his pupil's answer. The truth was that Tosu didn't have many leads on who had tried to ambush him and his men. Even though they were prepared for it and knew what was coming, Tosu and his team were no match for the skills of the two women and the men with them.

They'd lost many men. The enemy had only lost one, not counting Abdi.

"We will find them, Master, and they will suffer for their inso-lence," Tosu said before the older man could say anything else.

"Very well, Khalil," Shafir said, "Make certain they do. I would hate to have to...replace you."

"I do not wish that to—"

The line went dead. The leader hung up the phone before Tosu could finish his sentence.

Had it been someone beneath him, Tosu would have had the man killed right then and there for the rude gesture. It didn't work like that going up the chain of command. The Teacher had been the one to bring him in, give him a sense of purpose, and promise him the hope of immortality despite living a life of sin on this earth.

Tosu wasn't one for sentimentality. The real reason he wouldn't challenge the Teacher was that he couldn't. The man was an appari-tion, nothing more than a spirit that floated around the world, appearing and disappearing without warning.

He could have been anywhere on the planet at that moment. He might have even been calling from across the street. Tosu would have never known. The man was impossible to track down.

Of course, the way the Red Ring operated made sure that their leadership was never in the same place at the same time. That was a lesson they'd learned the hard way, when two of their clerics had met in a desert cave in the mountains of Afghanistan. The cave was bombarded in a surprise attack by (what they assumed to be) United States bombers.

The entrance had collapsed, and those inside were never heard from again. After that, the Red Ring made sure to keep their cells and their leaders a safe distance apart.

The only traceable thing about Shafir was his phone number, the one that appeared on the display of Tosu's phone. Sure, he could put one of his tech guys on it and have him try to trace the number, but if the Teacher found out, Tosu would be a dead man. Unlike all the soldiers who signed up for suicide missions on the Ring's behalf, Tosu had no desire to rush into death.

If he had to guess, he'd say that the old man definitely had safeguards in place to defend against such traces. More than likely, he'd ping the trace back to Tosu's guy, pinpoint his location, and firebomb the building before he could unplug.

There was no reason to take such action. Tosu was happy with his position. He had no desire to take over from the Teacher. That was a job for a holy man. Tosu wasn't ready to be holy just yet. The thought, combined with the irritation of being hung up on, triggered one of his carnal impulses.

"Amad!" he shouted.

One of his guards stepped in the room with a Heckler & Koch submachine gun slung over his shoulder.

"Yes, sir," the man said. The guy's shaved head was showing stubble that matched his beard.

"Bring me one of the girls."

"Of course, sir."

The guard started to leave. Tosu stopped him. "Amad."

The man reappeared in the doorway.

"Make that two."

# 8

DUBLIN

Adriana woke with a start. She looked around the unfamiliar room through a blurry film. She rubbed her eyes to clear them. Where was she? She didn't recognize the place.

She sat up, almost in a panic, and then remembered what happened. A-Tak's—rather, Ray's—apartment in Dublin. That's where she was. She took in the surroundings to get reacquainted. The simple, thin mattress on the futon had felt like sleeping on a cloud after the rigorous day she had yesterday. She'd underestimated how exhausted she really was. There wasn't even a memory of falling asleep. The last thing Adriana could recall was sitting on the edge of the couch while Ray was entering hundreds of lines of code to set up what he called his "net."

Her neck was a little stiff, which was another telling sign she'd slept hard during the night. That always happened when fatigue kept her in one place on the bed. She kept twisting it until there was a hint of relief and then stood up to get her blood circulating.

The little room was probably less than a hundred square feet. Tiny, undecorated, and surrounded in plain white walls, she wondered if her associate had ever set foot in the space.

She walked over to the door and cracked it open.

One of the hinges squeaked its protest as she looked out through the gap between the door and the frame.

Ray was sitting at his workstation, fingers flying across the keyboard. The sudden noise caught his attention, and he spun the chair around.

"Ah, good morning, sleepyhead," he said with a stupid grin.

Adriana frowned. She *was* a sleepyhead. *Another four hours should do the trick*, she thought, knowing full well that wasn't an option.

"How long was I out?" she asked, stepping into the living room.

He twisted to the left and grabbed a coffee mug next to his keyboard. "I dunno," he said with a shrug. "Eight hours? Maybe nine? I didn't time it."

"Crap."

"You were tired. You needed the sleep."

He sounded like her father. Diego Villa had always been a doting dad, almost to the point of spoiling her. It might have been the reason she'd pursued dangerous occupations and hobbies once she'd come of age. Deep down, she had the feeling he'd tried to keep her from that kind of life since his had been one of always looking over his shoulder.

"Coffee?" Ray asked.

She swallowed. Her throat was parched, and she could use some liquid, not to mention the caffeine. "How much you got?" she asked, half joking.

He grinned and stood up, walked over to the kitchen, and grabbed the steaming pot. Ray poured the coffee into a plain white mug. "Sugar or creamer?" he asked.

"Just a little sugar."

He grabbed a packet out of a bowl on the counter, stuck a spoon in the mug, and brought it over to her.

She took the hot brew gratefully and sipped, savoring it for a moment. She raised the mug and gave him an appreciative nod.

For a couple of seconds, her heart sank despite the toasty morning beverage in her hand. Adriana missed Sean. One of their favorite things to do together was wake up late and drink coffee.

They'd usually go through a few cups before heading off to start their day. Their coffee time gave them a chance to steal an extra hour from their hectic lives.

Now, not only was she running around the world, Adriana was chasing terrorists, one of the most dangerous things she could imagine doing.

But she wasn't afraid. Life had hardened her to most fears. That wasn't to say she never got scared. It was just that death wasn't the worst thing that could happen. Watching her mother die had relieved her of that fear. The agonizing moment her mother passed had burned into her memory, but Adriana also remembered the peace on her mother's face. The struggle was over. The torture would no longer continue. There was a kind of relief in that—for both mother and daughter. The memory was a fragment in time that took away her fears of dying and replaced them with a stoic resolve to live the best she could without worrying if the next day would come or not.

Ray slid back into his chair as she sidled up next to him on a stool. He noticed she was deep in thought, that or still waking up.

"So," he said, interrupting her thoughts, looking at all three monitors simultaneously, "we caught something interesting in the net last night."

Her eyebrows perked up. "Really?" Adriana was surprised although she knew she shouldn't be. He was good at what he did. That's why she was here. Still, Tosu was slippery. The entire Red Ring was an organization shrouded in a fog. No one knew how to get in. And finding those in charge was like finding a needle in a stack of needles.

"Yep."

She leaned forward, one elbow on a knee, taking another draft from the mug. Her eye ran over the lines of code on two of the screens. She didn't understand one bit of it. She wondered if her father, an agent well versed in methods outside the law, could have deciphered all the stuff Ray was looking at.

"How'd you do that? Did you put out some kind of search algorithm or something?"

He frowned for a second and then chuckled. "No. This is other stuff."

She cocked her head to the side and pinched her eyebrows together. "Then...how did you find them?"

"I put out a Craigslist ad for guns and explosives." He shrugged as he said it.

Her confused look deepened. "What?"

"I'm kidding. Although...it's kind of like that. I went on to the dark web and posted some fake ads for weapons, explosives, that kind of thing. Got a ton of hits from Russia, by the way. Whoever you're working for might want to look into them in the future. Just saying."

"Noted."

"We also got a lot from Eastern Bloc countries near there. Former Soviet countries are havens for hackers. Bad economies, lousy weather, and a chance to make some serious bank can cause people to bend their morals."

"You're one to talk."

"Hilarious," he said with a faux smile.

"How were you able to tell where the traffic is coming from?"

He raised an eyebrow. "Are you serious?"

Her head retreated an inch. "Yeah. Why?"

"Because, that's pretty simple. Have you ever heard of analytics?"

"Sure. On commercials for computer companies or businesses."

"Right," he said with a nod. "It's the same thing. Except on the dark web, you have to use a lot of different code. That's what I was doing last night when you saw me typing all that stuff. On the dark web, everyone is spying on everyone else. It's a cesspool of the worst kinds of people on the planet, so obviously you don't want other users to know you're tracking them. If they find out, they'll try to do the same to you."

"So, best practice is to stay as anonymous as possible."

"Exactly. I put in a bunch of barriers for anyone trying to worm their way back to us. Plus, there are tripwires in place to let us know if they get close."

"Tripwires?"

"It's like an alarm for your house, but for digital traces. If someone even thinks about trying to track down our location, we'll know about it."

She still had a ton of questions. Probably better to just save those for another time. As long as Ray was confident, so was she.

"So...other than the former Soviet states, I'm guessing you found something interesting?"

"Yes, but it wasn't from the information I put out there." Before she could ask, he answered the question hanging on her lips. "I also ran a program to hunt down anyone who's in the market for the kinds of things a terrorist might want, you know, the guns and things."

She nodded so he went on. "Then I cross-referenced it with the tracking data from the analytics. We got a few dozen matches, but only two of them look like they could be your guy."

"What's so special about those two?"

"I'm glad you asked," he said with a goofy smile. "There are a few things. One, those two shoppers offered hard currency."

Adriana knew what he meant by the term. They were most likely spending gold. Some people in the criminal underworld would take silver, but not usually. Gold was the preferred method of buying and selling. Unless it was marked, and based on her knowledge, it almost never was, gold was extremely difficult to trace.

Wire transfers and paper money were easier for the authorities to find. Paper less so once it was in the hands of the buyer or seller, but then it became difficult to spend. Physical money was tricky. It had to be laundered, filtered, and sifted through numerous channels before it came out clean on the other side. While the Red Ring probably had the resources for something like that, and used them on a day-to-day basis, someone offering gold was in a hurry.

"You said a few things," Adriana said, getting back to the subject.

"Right. I don't have to tell you why they'd use hard currency."

She appreciated that he gave her that much credit.

"The other reason I think one of these might be your guy is their location. One of them is in Pakistan. Definitely worth looking into. I don't have to remind you where we found Osama bin Laden."

Adriana knew about the Pakistani government's shady dealings in terrorism. She had a feeling there was more going on under the table, too. There were documented instances of them carrying out attacks in India. Their feeble attempts to conceal who the terrorists were working for did little to hide the truth. Then there were the missions conducted at the behest of Washington. Those, she hoped, were mere rumors, but something told her there was far more going on than what the public really knew.

The police and military did what they could to keep that from happening, but a few always slipped through the cracks. Border control for any nation larger than Lichtenstein would be difficult to maintain without flaw.

"And the other country?" she asked.

"Albania."

"Hmm. That's the one, then."

"Yeah, that's what I said. I mean, it's not totally shocking. I've seen some guys online before from there. That whole region was ravaged by that war back in the '90s, and even though most of the factions got their own countries out of it, there's still a lot of tension. The dudes I see online from there are usually doing the human trafficking thing, sometimes worse than that."

She wondered what could be worse and then decided she didn't want to know. "Albania would be a good place to hide out. And that's where Tosu is from. Although why would he go right back to his own backyard to avoid being found? That's a big risk."

"I leave that to you," he said. "I mean, you're the expert, right?"

Adriana pondered the results of Ray's efforts. Surely, Tosu wouldn't be brazen enough to go back to his own country, much less his own home. Right? Then again, sometimes the best place to hide was in plain sight, where no one would bother to look. She imagined several agencies must have some kind of intel on Tosu. He'd cut a pretty broad swath into the world, and his tracks couldn't be completely covered up.

"Can you get me an address?"

A printer on the left end of the workstation made a mechanical noise and then began running.

"Already did it," Ray said.

The paper slid out onto a tray. He picked it up and handed it to her with a proud look on his face.

She eyed the address, memorized it, and then stuffed it into her back pocket.

"So, I guess you'll be going?"

"Yes. I'll leave you alone...for now. You may resume whatever illegal activities you were doing before I got here."

"Thank you," he said with a hint of cynicism.

"No, thank you, Ra—I mean, A-Tak. I appreciate the help."

"You're quite welcome."

She grabbed her things and headed for the door. He walked her over and pulled it open to let her out. After she stepped out into the hall, she paused and turned around.

"Do me a favor," she said.

"You mean another one?"

"Yeah. Stop moving around so much. You know there's nowhere you can go I won't find you. So, next time, do us both a solid and stay here. Okay?"

Her eyes probed him to see how he'd take the request.

He simply grinned. "Now where's the fun in that?"

# 9

---

TIRANA

Adriana walked across the tarmac to the black sedan the agency had arranged. The driver exited and climbed into the passenger side of another car. The second sedan sped away a moment later, leaving her there alone.

June would be meeting her shortly at the rendezvous point—a hotel in the city. The room wasn't anything fancy, at least that's what she'd been told. They didn't want to draw any attention.

Adriana wore a simple outfit, jeans, a long-sleeved shirt, and a jacket over it. The air was chilly as it blew across the airfield, but not as cold as it'd been in Ireland.

She tossed her bag into the passenger seat and checked to make sure there was plenty of gas in the tank before leaving. Noting it was nearly full, she shifted it into gear and sped off, letting the GPS on the dashboard guide her into town.

Checking into the hotel was easy enough. Once she arrived, Adriana was greeted by a few valets, all of whom she ignored. No sense in having a couple of college-age boys looking through her stuff. She'd learned a long time ago that the valets in certain European countries were less than trustworthy.

She bypassed the valet station and drove around to the back of the building. Scaffolding along the wall on the side told her whoever owned the hotel was doing their best to give it some much needed upgrades, or at the very least a makeover.

After parking her car along a block wall just inside the property's perimeter, she made her way inside to check in and find the room.

While the shabby hotel exterior did little to bring patrons in on a random drive-by, the interior had already been overhauled. Were you to look at images of the outside and then the inside, you'd swear it was two different places.

Modern white fabric lights shaped like box kites hung from the ceiling in the center of the grand lobby. A concierge was perched behind his granite counter to the right. Three other identical spots were empty, telling Adriana this wasn't their busiest time of day...or year for that matter. The floor tiles looked like the same kind of granite used for the counters. Its shiny façade gave a luxurious feel to the place that it probably hadn't earned during its first decades in business.

The smell of jasmine wafted through the lobby, probably infused at several points by automatic air fresheners.

She'd noticed a similar scent in Las Vegas casinos, although Adriana knew that scent was also laced with higher levels of oxygen to keep the gamblers playing longer.

After getting her key, she made her way up to the room on the third floor and put her things down on the table by the window. As was her routine, Adriana opened her baggage and started taking inventory of her weapons, ammunition, and other tactical supplies. She'd checked it twice before getting in the car to the airport and then once more before boarding the plane. She believed you could never be too careful. It wasn't obsessive-compulsive. She simply preferred to be absolutely certain.

Being consistently persistent had saved her life in the past. She had no intentions of getting sloppy and dying anytime soon.

Satisfied that everything was as it should be, she zipped up the bag and slipped into the bathroom for a quick shower and a fresh set of clothes. Traveling—especially flying—always made her feel grimy.

Not to mention she had no idea when she'd be able to shower and change again.

The door to the room opened as she was leaving the bathroom, her hair still wrapped in a towel to dry. She grabbed her pistol and held it out, aiming low in case it was someone she knew. That way, the bullet would be less likely to kill and more likely to injure. A friend wouldn't appreciate either but would appreciate still being alive.

June's voice preceded her entry, saving Adriana the trouble of putting a round in her friend's abdomen.

"Adriana? It's me."

"Come on in," Adriana said, lowering the weapon as she walked over to the window.

June padded into the room and let the door close softly behind her. She noticed Adriana's hair in a towel. "Ugh," she said, "I always feel like I have to take a shower after traveling."

Adriana offered an understanding grin.

June plopped her small luggage bag on the bed and set her laptop case on the desk in the corner. "How long you been here?"

"Twenty minutes."

"Okay," June said. "Let me take a quick shower, and we'll get started."

Ten minutes later, June was in a fresh set of clothes and sitting at the desk with Adriana, staring at the computer screen.

"This is where our guy is." June tapped on the monitor. It displayed a map of the city. She circled one of the buildings with the same finger. "We believe he's holed up here right now."

"We believe?"

"Last our surveillance teams checked."

"When was that?"

"An hour ago."

"Oh," Adriana said, relieved. "Then yeah, he's probably still there. For a second it sounded like the last contact you had was a few weeks ago."

June chuckled and shook her head. "Anyway, he's likely there.

The building doesn't look well guarded." She twisted two fingers around on the screen, and the view changed to one from the street.

"Google doing real-time street views now?"

Another snicker escaped June's lips. "We have eyes all over the building now. Our team surrounded it when you gave me the location. They've had eyes on it 24/7. And by eyes I also mean cameras."

June shifted the view again, and the building's front door appeared on the screen. "Going in the front isn't an option."

"Heavily guarded?"

"Depends on what your definition of heavily guarded is. There are twelve guards on the other side of that door, each positioned in a different place so that if anyone comes through who isn't welcome, they'll be shot dead before they get to the elevator."

Adriana frowned, trying to comprehend what her partner had just said. "It's an apartment building? What about the other residents?"

"We believe the Red Ring owns the entire building. The rest of it is probably vacant."

Adriana raised an eyebrow, impressed. "They really are a well-funded organization, huh?"

"That's just the beginning. The elevators are key-code activated. If you don't know the correct code, you have to take the stairs. Good news: the stairs are also protected by a passcode."

"One that we don't have."

"Correct. So, that means we have to find another way in."

Adriana gave a slow nod. She had a feeling she knew what her friend was about to say next.

"This is where your unique set of skills comes into play," June said.

"I knew you were going to say that."

"Sorry to be predictable." June clicked the mouse pad and brought up another window. "These are the schematics to the entire building. We've discovered three other possible points of entry, but none of them are easy."

"Of course not."

"Path number one is a no-go. I was thinking we go in via the rooftop and then rappel down the side, bust through a window, and crash his penthouse."

"Why's that off the table?" Adriana asked.

"Tosu has men stationed on the roof. Six of them. They rotate shifts every two hours with another round of guards that patrol the hallways and stairs."

That was a lot of manpower to protect one guy. Adriana's eyebrows knit together. "Any idea how many guards we're talking about?"

"Like for the entire building?"

"Yeah."

June shook her head. "No, but we ballpark it around thirty at any given time. Could be more. Could be less."

Adriana knew it wouldn't be the latter. One thing she'd come to realize about these kinds of scumbags is that if they thought ten guards could do the job, twenty would be even better. Sure, it was overkill and maybe a bit more expensive, but for a group that had money to burn, why not? Could it be that Shadow Cell's admins had underestimated Tosu's importance? Anything was possible at this point.

"Okay, so, thirty guys," Adriana said. "A dozen in the lobby. Six on the roof. You said they rotate those six with others. That means six more in the corridors and stairwells."

"Which would leave six in Tosu's apartment."

"If your number is right. If it was me, I'd station two or three outside the door, or probably one at each end of the hallway and then two more inside his place."

"All right, so thirty."

"At least. He'll have half a dozen in his apartment. Then there are likely some stragglers somewhere else in the building. Or maybe positioned outside somewhere."

"Like I said, it's not gonna be easy," June said.

Adriana scanned the blueprints. She pressed her fingers to the screen and rotated the image, then twisted it to get a 3-D view.

"We could go in on zip lines and hit the roof that way. Would be close. I've got the gear for that, but when the grapple hits the building, it could alert the guards. What were the other two ways in you mentioned?"

"Unfortunately, they all involve the rooftop. It's the least guarded point of entry into the complex."

Six guards was hardly poorly guarded, but Adriana trusted her friend's assessment. It was her job to make calls like that. Now, apparently, it was Adriana's job to figure out a solution.

"Okay, so that means windows are one way in, stairwell is another, and I'm guessing your third option is...elevator shaft, accessed on the top floor?"

"Correct. All three pose different problems."

"Elevator shaft is the way to go, then."

"You're sure?"

Adriana gave a single nod. "They can't put men in that shaft. And truthfully, why would they think they needed to? To get in it, you'd have to get by all those guards. The stairs are no good because we don't know if there are men on the other side of the doors, or if they have guys stationed on the other side of the doors that come out of the stairwells. If I had to guess, I'd say someone is watching them."

June followed her friend's line of thought, and while she didn't disagree, she still had reservations. "Okay, so what happens if we go through the elevator shaft, manage to pry open the doors on Tosu's floor, and there are guards standing there?"

Adriana anticipated the question. She'd already run the scenario in her mind.

"Smoke canisters," she said. "I have a few in my bag. We use thermal scanners to detect movement on the other side of the wall. When and if we need to, we toss a few of those into the corridor. The guys won't know what hit them."

"That's an option. But the smoke will set off alarms, not to mention Tosu's men will go on full alert. They'll rally everyone to our location."

"Good point." It was something Adriana had considered but

thought it was the only option. Then she had another idea. "From the looks of it, the alarm system is pretty sophisticated."

"It is," June confirmed. "It's state of the art."

A wry smile creased Adriana's lips. "We're going to need some extra gear to get down into that elevator shaft. As for the security system, let me make a call."

# 10

TIRANA

"I really don't like this," June said.

The wind howled in her ears as she looked down from one of the tallest buildings in the city. It was almost midnight, and the city lights glowed bright against the dark backdrop of the sky.

She and Adriana were on the edge of Stadium Tower, 262 feet above the ground. They stood on the edge, with knees bent to keep their balance against the gusting wind.

"Sean would like it a lot less," Adriana quipped.

Sean's fear of heights was legendary. There was zero chance she'd get him onto a high ledge like this, not even for an important mission. He would have opted to find another way in. Probably through the front door with guns blazing.

She laughed internally at the mental image.

"It's gonna be fine," Adriana said. "Just make sure you throw your chute the second you're clear of the building. Our window is gonna be tight. Throw it too late, and you'll miss the landing spot."

The two women had parachute packs strapped to their back. They held the main chutes in their right hands. They were also armed with enough weapons and ammo to stage a small coup. Both carried a pistol on each hip, strapped down tight to keep the weapons from moving too much. In addition to the handguns, they carried HK-5 submachine guns tied tightly to their chests. They each had a complement of backup magazines for their weapons, with everything totaling over two hundred rounds.

Adriana would have carried more, but then she'd have sacrificed weight and agility for firepower. She knew her ability to move quickly was just as lethal as a bullet. Or so she hoped.

June cleared her throat. She'd never base-jumped before. Adriana hadn't either but assured her friend it would be fine. "Safer than jumping out of an airplane," she'd claimed.

June didn't need to know that was a lie.

"You ready?" Adriana asked, casting her partner a sidelong glance.

June shrugged. "Not really."

"Good. Remember, we'll be coming in pretty hot, so be sure you pump your legs as fast as you can when you get close to the rooftop."

June gave a tentative nod.

"I'll be right in front of you," Adriana reassured. Somehow, she knew it wasn't *that* reassuring.

She pressed a button on her lapel. "A-Tak, you ready to kill the lights?"

"Ready and waiting, boss."

Adriana had called on her associate for one more favor. Tosu's building was covered from head to toe in high-tech security systems and that, ironically, made them vulnerable to an online attack.

"Sixty seconds," Adriana said.

"Ten-four."

"Jumping now. Mark."

Adriana pushed off from the ledge and dropped away from the building. Air rushed by her, whistling loudly in her ears. She threw the black chute out as hard as she could, and the fabric caught air and yanked her upward.

She grabbed the handles and guided herself toward the target. The men on the rooftop were miniscule at first, but grew larger by the second. The area above Tosu's complex was well lit, with floodlights shining brightly from every corner. Adriana knew in a matter of seconds the rooftop would be bathed in darkness. Unless Ray screwed up.

If that happened, she and June would be cut down before they could put their feet on the ground. She considered the possibility and had decided that if the lights weren't killed within fifteen seconds of landing, she and June would abort and steer clear of the complex.

Even then, the guards would probably see them, which would make for a hairy escape amid a hail of gunfire.

A thousand yards from the target, Adriana pulled on both cords, and the parachute lifted slightly and steadied its course.

The city below her feet passed by quickly as she approached the target. The gap closed: nine hundred yards, eight hundred, seven hundred. Inside of five hundred yards, Adriana's concern ballooned. If Ray didn't kill the power, she and June would have to turn away.

"Come on, Ray," Adriana whispered to herself.

Five seconds passed like a month. Then suddenly, the bright lights on top of the building went dark.

The guards disappeared in the blackness, but Adriana could still make out the rooftop's silhouette against the glittering backdrop of the city.

"Good man, Ray," she said.

A hundred yards and closing quickly, Adriana readied herself for impact. She raised her feet like she'd been trained to do on her first jump from an airplane. Her boots cleared the roof ledge with ten feet to spare, and she let off on the cords to allow the chute to go limp.

Her feet hit the ground and she rolled forward. It took her less than two seconds to cut the chute free and draw the pistol from her hip. The suppressor on the end of the barrel made freeing the gun a little clumsier than normal, but it was essential to keep things quiet.

The parachute fluttered away in the gusting wind and a moment later disappeared over the edge.

June hit the ground and rolled fifty feet away from Adriana. She deftly copied her partner's movements, pulling her weapon and freeing herself from the chute.

Adriana saw one of the guards appear around a huge air conditioning unit. He was chattering on a walkie-talkie about the power outage, ordering someone to get the lights back on.

The man was between the two women as he walked over to the edge and looked out.

Adriana started to sneak in his direction but sensed something move behind her. She ducked under a huge ventilation cylinder and waited for a second. A guard appeared around the corner, pacing deliberately to where she'd just been standing.

"Did you see that?" he said into his radio, cutting off the guy who was in the middle of a rant about the power outage.

"See what?"

Adriana sprang from her hiding spot with knife drawn. She plunged the tip into the base of the man's skull and drove it up into his brain. His body shuddered for a second and then went limp. She withdrew the blade and let him fall to the ground, dead instantly.

She looked across the rooftop and saw June pulling her knife's edge across the other guard's throat. The man waved his arms around for a moment and then desperately clutched his neck to stem the bleeding. He fell to his knees and then lay prostrate on the ground in a pool of dark crimson.

Adriana made a signal for June to go around the other way to sweep the perimeter. They'd discussed the plan ahead of time, and both women knew to take out as many of the bad guys as possible as they worked their way to the middle, where the maintenance door led to the elevator.

Two down. Four to go.

June spun around and took off in the other direction, crouching low behind a row of air conditioning units as she made her way to the corner of the building.

Adriana turned and crept behind a huge machine. It was a tangled mess of pipes and hoses. What the thing was for, she had no idea, but it gave her cover as she skirted the rooftop in search of her next target.

A burst of radio static from the other side of the machine gave away another guard's position. Adriana moved with graceful speed. She rounded the machine's backside and caught a glimpse of the guard's jacket as he stalked down the row toward where she'd been just a moment before. In a couple of seconds, he'd find the bloody body of his associate and radio for help.

He was already checking in on the patrol with his walkie-talkie. No doubt, he was heading that direction because it was the last place the dead guard had responded.

Adriana snuck around, knife ready to give him the same treatment as the first guy.

She was so focused on the target that she didn't notice a strip of thick gray wire running from the machine on her right to another unit on the left. Her boot caught it, and she lost her balance for a fraction of a second.

The stumble caused her left foot to pound the surface of the roof hard. The noise startled the guard and he spun around with his submachine gun leveled, waist high.

The knife wasn't an option now.

Adriana raised her pistol and fired a quick burst of three muffled shots. One of them missed, smashing into the short wall surrounding the roof. The other two struck true, hitting the target in the chest. She left nothing to chance, rushing to the falling man and planting one more round in his skull before he fired his weapon and alerted the city.

She hovered over him for a second. His lifeless eyes stared into the twinkling night sky above.

"Patrol five, come in," a man's thick accent came through the radio. "Where are two and three? Is something wrong with their radios?"

She picked up the walkie-talkie attached to the guy's vest and clipped it to her belt, turning the volume down a few notches before she started back toward the middle of the roof.

She listened intensely, hoping her third mark would reveal his location, but the radio had gone silent. At least the guy wasn't putting the entire building on alert.

Adriana stayed low, moving with ninja-like stealth as she reached the end of the row. There was no one standing on the path between her and the elevator shaft entrance. Her eyes narrowed with suspicion. Where was the guard?

She didn't see any sign of June, either, which was concerning. June should have also been making her way toward the elevator shaft.

Suddenly, a big arm wrapped around her neck and squeezed.

The man's dense forearm crushed her throat and cut off the air to her lungs. Adriana felt her eyes bulging out of their sockets almost instantly. She kicked and wiggled to free herself, but the man lifted her off the ground, leaning his body back for leverage. Her feet swung wildly. Her head turned back and forth but couldn't move more than a half inch or so due to the big man's brute strength.

He dragged her backward, passing the machine with all the pipes, and slowed his pace until she realized where he was taking her. He wasn't going to choke her to death. He was going to throw her over the edge.

# 11

TIRANA

The huge guard twisted his body, moving Adriana's feet out over the ledge. A terrifying vision of falling to the pavement below filled her mind. For the first time in her life, she understood Sean's fear and did everything in her power to escape the man's death grip.

A low pop interrupted her thoughts. The sound came from the left. Almost instantly, the guard's arms went limp. She felt herself falling, but luckily the guard was toppling backward. Her butt hit the ground by the big man's knee, and she rolled to the side, ready to fight him if he wasn't yet dead.

The bullet hole in his left temple did away with that potential problem. Adriana tried to swallow, but it was difficult. She knew her throat would be sore for a few days. As she caught her breath, she saw a shadow approaching. It wasn't a threat. It was June holding her pistol at her side.

"Thought you could use a little help."

"Thank you," Adriana managed. "Glad he fell backward."

June bit her lower lip. "Yeah, had to take a gamble on that."

"Other guards dead?" Adriana asked, not wanting to harp on her near-death experience for long.

June gave a nod. "Yeah, they're taken care of."

Adriana tried not to show her surprise, but she was impressed. This wasn't the first mission she and June had worked together on, but the natural, almost callous killer instincts June displayed—along with precision—had caught Adriana a tad off guard.

"Good," she said, not wanting to delay further. "Let's get to the shaft."

They hurried over to the maintenance access. It was nothing more than a metal rectangular box with a side door about four feet high. A padlock on the clasp was the only thing keeping people out, although Adriana couldn't imagine why anyone would want to get in there—unless they had a death wish or were just stupid.

She reached into a cargo pocket and pulled out a small device. It looked like a cigar lighter, but was much more than that. It had two black prongs that rose up from the main body. Within those prongs were four metal rods. She placed one of the padlock bars inside the prongs and pressed a button on the center of the gadget. The prongs turned bright orange. Suddenly, the padlock glowed a similar color. A few seconds later, the thing fell from its hinge to the ground, the bar melted from the plasma lighter.

June swung the door open and leaned inside. She couldn't see much in the pitch-dark shaft. The rooftop lights came back on and startled the two women, though they knew that was going to happen. Ray's mischief was designed to keep the power down for only a few minutes to make it look natural.

"Rooftop patrol, do you copy?" A voice came through the radio on Adriana's belt.

"Crap," she said and grabbed the device. She made static noises and then used the manliest voice she could muster. "Copy...power back on. Sweeping area now."

There was a pause. June and Adriana exchanged a concerned look for a moment while they waited for the guy to respond.

They were flooded with relief when he came back on the radio. "Copy that."

Adriana sighed. Learning Arabic was turning out to be one of the best investments of time she'd ever made.

June reached into a cargo pocket and pulled out a metal disc. On one side, the thick device had a digital readout and three buttons. The spool contained a thin cable, capable of holding four hundred pounds, although she had no intentions to test that strength. Adriana also pulled a similar disc from her pants and tapped the buttons.

"How far down?" she asked.

"Tosu is on the top floor. It's only a thirty-foot drop. Of course, if these things don't work, the drop could be much farther depending on where the lift is right now."

The answer didn't exactly fill Adriana with confidence, but she'd been in tight spots before—worse ones, actually.

They clipped their harnesses onto a hook on the end of the spool and then reached around the inside of the portal's frame and attached the magnetic discs to a steel support beam. Then they pressed a button on the right, and the device switched on, indicated by a red light. Seconds later, the light turned green.

Adriana pressed a button with a plus arrow until the blue digital display read 30. Then she looked over at her partner. "Ready?"

June finished the same process and then nodded. "Ready if you are."

Adriana gave a nod and then swung her right leg out over the abyss. She held on to the cable with both hands and sat back away from the opening for a moment to test its stability. It seemed to hold just fine, so she stood up and eased herself into the darkness.

She planted her feet against the wall, leaning back to rappel down. June tested her line and then joined her friend in the shaft. She reached up and pressed a button. Adriana did the same.

It only took two seconds for the devices to start letting out the slack on the line. The women used the balls of their feet to keep control of their descent. Once they were ten feet down, it was nearly impossible to see anything. The only light in the shaft was coming from the maintenance door above, and that wasn't much.

They kept moving at a steady, cautious pace.

At twenty feet, it was pitch black. The portal at the top did almost nothing down that far.

When the women hit the thirty-foot mark, the motor in the discs stopped. Adriana reached into a cargo pocket and found a pair of glasses. She slid them onto her nose and flipped a tiny switch on the right temple. The lenses changed to a greenish color, and suddenly the elevator shaft illuminated before her eyes.

The door into Tosu's floor was right in front of them.

June reached into one of her pockets and retrieved a thin plastic box with a camera lens on one side. She pressed its prong into the female power adapter on her phone and then hit the power button.

Her phone's screen lit up, showing nothing but dim, bleak space. Then she turned it to the left. Nothing. She swung carefully to the right.

Adriana watched her partner. June pointed to the right corner of the elevator shaft and then held up two fingers.

Two figures appeared on her phone screen in bright red, orange, and yellow. The thermal scanning device was capable of detecting heat signatures from up to a hundred feet. Inside the elevator shaft would limit that range, but it was apparently still effective. June twisted around again to recheck the other end of the hall. It remained empty.

Adriana reached back to her belt and produced another tool with what looked like pliers on the end. She inserted the narrow end into the seam in the center of the elevator doors. Then she turned a rod sticking out of the top. The doors parted slightly. Adriana cranked the rod several times until the opening was around five inches wide. The bright light from the hallway seared her vision for a second, and she had to turn off the lenses to save her eyes.

She squinted hard, squeezing her eyelids to adjust to the light. It took a few seconds. Then she was back to work, prying the door open.

June continue scanning the hallway with her device. She turned to the right and saw the figures of the two guards still positioned where they had been before. Then she swung back to the left. No sign of...wait. A new figure appeared on the screen, walking down the hall toward them.

Her heart rate quickened.

She reached over and tapped Adriana's shoulder then showed her the screen. The guard was bearing down on them at a steady pace.

Adriana sighed and twisted the rod the other direction to allow the elevator doors to close. It didn't work. Instead, the doors remained open, and her tool came loose, nearly dropping from her hand into the darkness below.

She swallowed and then shoved the tool back into her pocket.

Neither woman panicked, but they were far from relaxed at this point.

The guard would be in front of the door within ten seconds.

Adriana had an idea. She didn't dare say a word lest the guard hear them. Her idea, however, was risky anyway. But it was the only thing she could think of. She couldn't close the elevator doors. And the guard would absolutely see that they were open and assume something was wrong. He'd probably stick his head in and have a look around. When that happened, the jig would be up.

Adriana stuck a hand on each door and pulled. She didn't want to fling them open abruptly. That would draw attention, too. So she inched the doors open wide enough that she could fit through.

June wasn't given to panic often, but at the sight of her friend pulling the elevator doors open wider she felt a wave of concern rush over her. She put out her free hand as if asking what in the world Adriana was doing, but her partner didn't respond until she was satisfied with the width of the gap.

Then Adriana turned to June and motioned for her to get back. June scowled but did as ordered. She grabbed a metal support beam along the wall and pulled herself back, using her feet to brace her weight. Adriana did the same, withdrawing to the corner of the shaft and pulling her knife from the sheath on her thigh.

When the guard appeared just outside the elevator shaft, June stuffed the phone back in her pocket and waited. Both women held their breath as the man's shadow appeared in the corridor.

June desperately wanted to know what Adriana was thinking. She didn't have to wait long to find out.

The guard paused outside the opening. The women couldn't see the curious, confused look on his face. His shadow drew near until they could see the tips of his shoes.

Adriana held the knife tight. She knew precision was a must, otherwise the other two guards at the end of the hall would be alerted. If that happened, she and June would find themselves in a gunfight with nowhere to hide and nowhere to run.

The guard leaned forward, exposing the top of his head. He tentatively looked down into the shaft, clearly wary of the danger. Adriana waited, forcing herself to be patient. He hadn't spotted them, instead enamored of the deadly drop before him.

He craned his neck a little more, keeping his balance by planting his hands on either side of the doorway.

That was all Adriana needed.

She pushed off from the side wall and swung toward the guard. In the darkness, he didn't detect any movement until it was too late. His head snapped toward her. Adriana drove the knife tip through the man's chin and up through the roof of his mouth. The sharp point tore through his sinuses and an instant later, his brain. He only managed a gurgle before his body went limp. Adriana yanked the blade free as the man fell forward, tumbling down the shaft into the blackness below. He hit the lift with a thud. How far down, the women didn't know. They also didn't care.

June pulled out her device and switched it back on. The two guards at the other end hadn't seen what happened. Adriana's kill had been swift and stealthy.

Now it was time to take out the rest of the guards and nab Tosu.

**Tirana**

JUNE SWUNG into the opening and pressed her toes onto the floor where thin carpet met the edge of the elevator's threshold. The cable went slightly limp, and she unclipped the harness. Adriana hung by, waiting for her friend to get unhooked. When June was free of the cable, Adriana stepped onto the ledge and removed the carabiner from her harness.

She stuffed the knife back in the sheath and drew a pistol.

June did the same and gave a nod that signaled she was ready.

They both knew the guards were standing watch over Tosu's corner penthouse. It was why they hadn't moved yet. The women were lucky they hadn't noticed their comrade disappearing into the elevator shaft, otherwise the gunfight would already be on.

The two targets were fifty feet away, standing on either side of the door to Tosu's apartment. The one on the left—closest to the women —was looking to his right, out a window that exposed a section of the city.

Adriana picked up her pace, walking as fast as she could without making much noise. June stayed close by, weapon behind her back.

At twenty-five feet, the guard nearest them turned his head and saw them approaching. The blonde and the brunette were quite the visual, both decked out in black tactical gear, submachine guns strapped to their chests, pistols on their hips, and a threatening look on both their faces.

The guard turned to face them, reaching for a gun in a side holster.

His reaction was much too slow. Adriana whipped her pistol up and fired three shots. The bullets smashed into the man's neck, shoulder, and skull, dropping him to the floor in an instant.

The second guard twisted around in time to see two suppressor muzzles flashing accompanied by a familiar muffled popping sound.

The rounds tore through his torso and limbs, piercing vital organs and smashing bone. His body shuddered with every bullet strike. He staggered backward and hit the window with a thud before falling facedown on the floor.

Adriana and June sped up, rushing over to the door. They stopped for a second to make certain the two guards wouldn't be getting up again. The two men were lying perfectly still, the carpet under them soaking up the thick red liquid leaking from their bodies. A quick check told the women neither man had a pulse.

Adriana reached into a pocket and pulled out a small cylinder. The thing fit in the palm of her hand. She gave a nod to June, who returned the gesture, understanding what would come next.

They took a step back and charged the door, simultaneously driving the heels of their boots into it. The portal caved under their combined weight and force. It flew open with a shudder.

As they followed their momentum into the apartment, June raised her weapon while Adriana tossed the flashbang inside. Then they stepped back out and waited. It only took a second for the device to explode. A bright flash of light escaped the apartment. They'd decided on flashbangs since smoke grenades would do as much to hinder their vision as it would an enemy's. Flash grenades, on the other hand, would blind a target for nearly a minute, burning their eyes with a searing light.

Then Adriana plunged ahead, sweeping the kitchen to her left with the pistol in her hands. June took the right. A short hallway led to a bathroom on one side and an office on the other. Straight ahead, the living room was shrouded in a light haze from the small amount of smoke the flashbang put out.

There were, however, no enemies to be found.

Adriana moved forward with purpose. She scanned the guest bedroom back on the left and found it to be empty. A quick check in the closet revealed the same.

She looked back through the doorway at June, who was checking the master bedroom on the other side of the enormous villa. Then Adriana's eyes went up the stairs to the loft above. She crept out of the guest room and made her way quietly over to the steps. One at a time, she climbed the stairs, pausing at the top in case someone was lying in wait to ambush her.

No one was there.

A desk sat along the loft wall. A plush white couch was positioned in front of a big high-definition television.

But no one was there, either.

Adriana poked her head over the railing and looked down as June reappeared from the master suite.

"It's empty," she said.

June had a confused look on her face. "Same down here. I don't understand. Our surveillance team said Tosu came in last night and never left. If he did, we'd have known it."

*Where was everyone?* Adriana kept the question to herself. She lowered her weapon and descended the stairs quickly.

A sudden, horrifying realization struck her.

"We need to leave. Now."

She turned toward the door. A man was standing in the way with a pistol held waist high. She recognized him immediately.

"How nice of you girls to drop by," Tosu said in a cool, wicked tone. "Speaking of drop, please drop that gun of yours."

June turned and saw the terrorist. She couldn't do anything. Adriana was squarely in his sights, and was just as vulnerable standing to the side by a black leather couch.

"You, too," Tosu said to June. "Or I can go ahead and shoot your friend right now."

June hesitated for a second.

"Don't do it, June," Adriana ordered. "The second he fires, drop him."

Tosu cocked his head to the side and displayed a sinister, cynical grin. "Really? Do you honestly think that will save her? You obviously don't see what happened here."

Adriana narrowed her eyes.

Tosu flicked his head, motioning for them to look out the giant wall windows facing the city. "Go ahead. Have a look."

Adriana reluctantly twisted her head enough to see outside. June looked, too. Four men dressed in the same gear as the other guards were hanging outside the window with submachine guns pointing into the villa.

"You see?" Tosu said. "There's nowhere for you to go. Now, if you don't mind, drop your guns, or I'll make this much more painful for the both of you."

June sighed and let her pistol drop to the floor. Adriana waited a few extra seconds before she complied. Her weapon struck the hardwood surface with a thud and a clank.

"That's better."

He took a short step back, and four armed guards poured into the room. They surrounded the women, keeping their weapons trained on the intruders.

"I'm glad to see my little trap worked."

Adriana's nostrils flared. Her eyes blazed with a fire hotter than a thousand suns. She did little to try to hide her anger.

"How did you know?" June asked, not expecting an honest answer.

"Please," Tosu said as he stepped into the villa. "Did you really think I didn't know about your little surveillance team? We have security systems in place that detect that kind of thing. Although I'm not surprised. You agency types are always a step behind. You mistakenly believe that all of us are hiding out in caves somewhere, living like animals."

One of the guards busied himself with disarming the women. It took a moment since they still had knives, guns, and full magazines strapped to them. The guard tossed their collection of weapons and ammo onto the couch and then returned to his place, keeping an eye on the prisoners.

"What did you do with them?" June asked. There was an intense concern in her tone.

"With who?" Tosu asked. He feigned innocence.

"You know who. Where are they? Where's the surveillance team? So help me, if you hurt any of them—"

"Why don't you look for yourselves?" he interrupted.

June frowned. For a second, she couldn't tell if the man was looking at her or over her shoulder. Then she followed his gaze to the window. The guards who'd been dangling from ropes had climbed back up to the top, revealing a clear view of the city once more.

"Look at what?" June asked. She wasn't sure she wanted the answer. It came suddenly and with terrible brutality.

A body fell from above and jerked suddenly. The rope around the man's neck snapped the bone within instantly. The body twitched, toes kicked, but the man was already dead, his neck broken.

"No!" June shouted, recognizing the guy as one of the team responsible for watching Tosu's compound.

Another body dropped, this one a woman with brown hair. The rope went taut and killed her instantly.

"Stop it! Please!" June begged.

Adriana could do nothing but watch as two more bodies, another man and woman, fell from the rooftop. The four members of the surveillance team hung in front of the window, their corpses twisting and turning in full macabre view of everyone in the penthouse.

June spun around, ready to pounce, but she had nowhere to go, no weapon to use. "You monster!" she shouted.

Tosu took a menacing step forward. "Monster? You send your soldiers into my land, execute my people, rape and murder those who are loyal to the true god, and yet you have the gall to call me a monster? No. You are the monsters. America and its allies are the ones responsible."

He reached out and grabbed her face, squeezing both sides of her jaw with strong fingers. He forced her head around. "Look at them," he said. "They are dead because of you. They are dead because your governments tried to stop us. Nothing can stop us. No one can stop us. And soon, the world will know who the true villains are. They will see that our cause is righteous, and with Allah on our side none can stand in our way until the earth has been purified."

"You missed the point," Adriana said out of the blue.

Tosu turned and glared at her as he would have a child who'd spoken in class without raising their hand. "What did you just say?"

"I said you missed the point," she answered without hesitation.

He took a step closer to her, releasing June's face as he moved. "Oh? And what point is that?"

"Allah doesn't want this. He doesn't want any of this. You make good people look bad. Because of trash like you, Muslims in free countries are discriminated against. They're treated like outsiders, weirdos, or killers. Because of people like you, women can't wear their hijabs into an airport without raising alarms inside the minds of thousands. Is that what you think Allah wants? Because it isn't. You've twisted the message of the almighty and turned it into a declaration of war. That's not what he wanted."

Tosu listened patiently until she was done talking. Then he pouted his lips as if considering the point. Then his left hand suddenly jerked around, and he backhanded her across the cheek. The ring on his finger opened a cut below Adriana's right eye.

Her head snapped to the side, but she didn't give him the pleasure of hearing her cry out. She winced for a second against the sting, but that was all.

"You know nothing of the true god," he said in a rage. "But you will soon. The entire world will bow before us, and then they will know the truth. Or they will die."

# 12

TIRANA

Adriana and June were loaded into the back of a cargo van along with the four guards who'd accompanied Tosu and helped him spring his trap. They never took their eyes off the two women. Likewise, Adriana and June probed the men for any weakness they could exploit. Even the smallest mistake could be fatal in the hands of those two.

During the entire bumpy journey out of the city, the men never once faltered. They were, apparently, well trained and highly disciplined. Adriana had to wonder who they were, what they'd been through to reach that kind of callous stoicism.

She'd never served in the military, but she'd heard stories. The American Marine Corps was tough. Parris Island was no vacation spot. Sand fleas nicked at the Marines' skin as they stood at attention in the sweltering South Carolina heat. The humidity doubled the misery. All the while, the would-be Marines were pushed to their physical limitations.

The best of the best would go higher, into tougher training. The military had several special operations divisions, each one presenting a test of will like the recruits had never seen in their lives.

Through those trials, fiercely determined, disciplined warriors were born.

As Adriana stared across the truck at one of the guards, she could see that kind of experience written on his face.

Maybe he'd been in his country's military. It was difficult to tell his origin. He had a strong, broad jaw, was slightly tanned, and had short black hair on his head. He and the other guards never said a word. They just stared at their prisoners through dead, vapid eyes. Wherever the guards had come from, whatever their past, one thing was certain: they were trained killers.

Adriana cursed herself for being so easily baited into a trap. Tosu's move had been clever. He'd banked on the idea that whoever was watching him didn't know he knew. It was the correct assumption.

Adriana figured June was likewise beating herself up for not being more wary of some kind of ambush. Truth was, neither one of them could have known what was going to happen.

June wore a bewildered look on her face like a mask of shame. Adriana knew her friend was carrying the deaths of the four operators on her shoulders. She could see the pain hanging on June, weighing her down. While Adriana knew her friend was a professional, she also couldn't imagine what that kind of responsibility felt like. She'd never want that on her conscience. Now, June had to live with it for the rest of her life.

The truck slowed, the inertia of the occupants pushing them toward the front for a moment before the vehicle made a slow right turn. Fifteen seconds later, the brakes squealed again, and the truck came to a stop.

The back door rattled as someone outside unhooked the clasp keeping it in place. Then the big door slid up into the truck's ceiling. Four men stood outside, all armed with submachine guns and pistols at their sides. A fifth man was standing just behind them, like a dog walker keeping his charges on a leash. The guards in the truck stood immediately. One of them grabbed June by the shoulder and forced her to her feet. Another did the same to Adriana and then pushed her toward the opening.

Their hands were bound with duct tape wrapped tightly around the wrists. The men who'd done the binding weren't stingy with the sticky material. They'd left nothing to chance with these two.

The women were ushered out of the truck, and after a few seconds their eyes adjusted to the new surroundings.

They were on the side of a titanic mountain in the range Adriana had admired upon first arriving in Tirana. Below, the plains stretched out as far as the eye could see. The city of Tirana twinkled in the dark of night, mirroring the stars above.

"Take them inside," Tosu ordered.

Someone shoved Adriana in the lower back, and she lurched forward. The hand steered her around the truck to the left. That's when she saw the building.

It didn't look like much. Other than being big, probably taking up four thousand square feet, it was also three stories tall. The walls were covered in rusty metal, as was the roof. Adriana wondered what the old building was, thinking it looked similar to abandoned mining structures she'd seen in the American Southwest.

The women were marched up a gravel driveway where the guards paused at the door. One of them rapped three times. A slide panel opened in the center of the portal. Pale eyes stared out from a dark, grimy face. Then the opening shut and locks started clicking inside. A moment later, the door groaned its protest as the man inside pulled it open.

Adriana and June stepped inside, following four of the men. The building had a dusty, metallic scent.

Ancient mining carts sat on old tracks that disappeared into a tunnel boring into the mountain. Huge racks, full of automatic guns and larger weapons, like RPGs, lined the walls. From a rapid assessment, Adriana figured there had to be a few thousand guns in the room. And that was just one area.

Rusty metal stairs ascended to a second floor where a catwalk wrapped around the center of the building. More stairs went up to the third floor, but it was difficult to see what was there. Men in black clothing were scurrying around as if preparing for something. Adriana had a bad feeling about whatever it was they were doing. No chance it was going be good. These men were bent on bringing death to the innocent, taking away life, liberty, and the pursuit of anything remotely decent. They had enough weapons and ammunition to start a small war or, in their case, wreak havoc on society.

So much for gun control in this country. Apparently it wasn't something the Albanian government cared to stem. Or maybe Tosu simply had them in his back pocket. Either way, the man appeared to be planning something big.

The door slammed shut behind them, startling the prisoners.

Adriana and June both looked back and saw Tosu surrounded by guards. He stared at the women for a moment before addressing them. He stepped by them with long, deliberate strides and then spun around when he was between them and the mining carts. His hands went out wide as if showing off a new home to special guests.

"Do you like it?" he asked. There was a hint of pride in his voice that only someone who craved destruction could appreciate.

"Looks like you've been busy," Adriana said.

"You could say that."

"It also looks like you're planning something big," she added.

"Very astute of you. Of course, I'm sure you'd love to know what that is, but you'll have to wait and see with the rest of the world."

First clue. Whatever the Red Ring was getting ready to do, it would be on a grand scale.

No doubt all the major news outlets would be covering it. It was a downside to the modern world. Everything went viral in a matter of seconds. Videos were streamed by millions every minute. The moment something bad happened, news channels were on the scene, sharing the horrors and tragedy with the planet.

It was one of the reasons Adriana never watched the news. She couldn't take it. Only Sean and a few of her close friends knew that about her. On the outside, she was as tough as the proverbial nail. On the inside, however, bloomed a delicate flower that cared deeply for the good of mankind. It was one of the reasons she'd set out to right the wrongs of World War II and the thievery that had been carried out by the Nazis.

Now she was in a bind. There was no doubt Tosu and his men would torture her and June. They would do whatever it took to extract who they were, who they worked for, and what the agency was planning next.

The terrorists wouldn't get what they wanted. Adriana knew that much. It was the only card she and June had left to play—defiance.

"You're gonna need a lot more than this if you want to take down the free world, Khalil," June said through clenched teeth. Her words were lathered in fury.

Tosu flashed a toothy grin. "Oh, I'm well aware of that. This is just the beginning. Take them down," he said to one of the guards.

The man immediately shoved June in the back, guiding her toward the mining tunnel. Adriana was pushed into line right behind her.

The group marched into the corridor that had been bored into the mountain long ago by men seeking their fortunes. Dusty wires lined the rock walls, running into a light every twenty feet or so before continuing their seemingly unending journey deeper into the mine.

They walked for what seemed like an hour, though in reality it was only ten minutes, until they arrived at a crossroads in the path. The train tracks forked in three directions. One set went farther into the tunnel ahead. The other two split to the right and left. The curves in the tracks were merged with a manual handle jutting up from the base to the right so miners could change directions easily when they arrived at the junction.

"What did they mine here?" Adriana asked, figuring it couldn't hurt anything to have a friendly conversation.

She didn't see Tosu raise a curious eyebrow at the question. He was three guards back, bringing up the rear. "Gold, originally. They found a few veins of it here long ago, but not much. The thing that brought most of the money was bauxite. The original owners of this property stripped it clean. When the bauxite was gone, they moved on to other things and left the mine as you see it now."

Adriana had seen a bauxite mine before. She'd been on a hike with Sean in the hills of Southern Tennessee and stumbled across tracks and carts similar to the ones in this mine.

She didn't say anything else to Tosu, instead letting the corridor fall into a tense silence.

The men led them down the passage to the left. The tunnel opened wider, providing enough room for the guards to walk four across if they wanted. Up ahead, sounds of metal grinding echoed off the roughly hewn rock. Hammers, drills, sanders, welders, and other tools caused it to sound like a big-city construction zone rather than an abandoned mine.

It didn't take long for them to learn where the sounds were coming from.

The corridor widened toward the mouth and led into a gigantic room. The place wasn't a natural cave; that much was clear. Steel support beams ran along the ceiling, grounded with huge concrete bases that must have gone ten feet into the earth.

The room looked like Santa's workshop for terrorists.

Workers were busy making bullets, assembling weapons, and constructing explosives. Adriana had heard of terrorist camps before. Usually, they were out in the middle of nowhere, covered with sand-colored camouflage netting to keep satellites and planes from spying on their activities, or in some cases, finding them to begin with.

This, however, was no ordinary terrorist camp. It was an assembly line of death.

Something caught Adriana's eye on the other side of the giant chamber. A separate group of men were working in white lab coats. There were several large tables. On top of them was the unmistakable shape of rockets. Beyond the tables, a steel door had been fitted into the wall. There was a reinforced window set into it, but she couldn't see beyond. Adriana didn't need to look through it to have an educated guess as to what it might be.

"Germ warfare?" she asked, though it was more of a statement in her tone.

Tosu only offered a stupid grin in response as he tilted his head back. That was answer enough.

"So," June said, "you're building dirty bombs. You realize that in the free world we have the resources to knock out that kind of stuff, right?"

Tosu put his hands behind his back and raised up on his tiptoes for a second. Then he lowered himself down slowly. "Ah, you must be talking about your Patriot missiles and their newest iterations."

June neither confirmed nor denied.

"Well, you'll be glad to know that these midrange weapons are equipped with jamming and cloaking devices. The latter makes it nearly impossible to detect on radar, while the former scrambles a hard lock any antiaircraft missile would utilize. So far, our tests have shown an increase of 120 percent accuracy over previous weapons."

"Like the Scuds Saddam Hussein tried to use?"

He let out a laugh. "My dear, that was so long ago. Your government really needs to update their information if that's what you think I'm comparing it to."

June bit her lip.

"Now that you've had the tour...." He turned to one of the guards. "Lock them in their cells."

Adriana frowned. She wondered when the interrogation was going to begin. One guard grabbed her left arm just under the shoulder. Another took the right in the same way. Their strong fingers felt like vice grips squeezing her muscles.

"I don't know what you think you're going to get out of us," June said. "But we won't tell you anything. You might as well kill us and get it over with."

Tosu nodded as if contemplating her statement. "Oh, I know I'm not going to get any useful information out of the two of you." He leaned forward like he was about to share a deeply intimate secret. "The bad news for you two is I don't need any information you could give me. I don't care what agency you work for, what country. I don't even care who you are, so spare me the whole speech about not telling me what I want to know. I don't want to know anything."

June frowned. "Then what are we doing here?"

He rolled his shoulders. "You're the enemy. And more than that, you're a heathen, scum of the earth. You and all the other nonbelievers must be purified by fire. Part of that purification is watching everything you stand for burn to the ground."

That was a little dark. Adriana didn't know anyone who thought like that—well, no one sane. Now it was starting to make sense. Tosu wanted the two of them to sit and watch while his men carried out their next attack. Perhaps after they'd been forced to view the destruction they would be given the comfort of death. Adriana doubted it would be that simple. They, no doubt, would be forced into a few other disgusting actions before finally receiving a bullet to the head as their prize.

She could sense the way the men in the room were looking at them. The pervasive sense was that their expressions were both disdainful and full of lust. There was no telling how long they'd been down here, not to mention how long since they'd seen a woman. Surely they lived in the city and had somewhat normal lives. Then again, the way most terror cells operated consisted of a lonely life, one that required an absence from society so the soldiers could focus on their primary objective. They prided themselves outwardly by professing chastity and total allegiance to Allah. The truth was they engaged in wretched behaviors, often turning the camp into a lewd scene more befitting a maximum security prison.

Adriana shook off the thought. No sense in getting worked up about something that hadn't happened yet. That was the beautiful thing about the future; it wasn't written in stone.

The guards ushered them across the room to another steel door set between two high shelves. The storage spaces were filled with parts for guns, makeshift explosives, and any number of other things. Wires, bits of metal, ball bearings, and several tubes were strewn about.

Adriana half wondered how the members of the Red Ring hadn't blown themselves up as a result of their carelessness. One wrong wire, an incorrectly placed chip, and one of those rockets would go boom and take out every man inside.

She snuck one last glance at the men working on the weapons as the guard in front opened the door to their cell. June was shoved inside first, then Adriana. The door was slammed shut, leaving the two women inside with a few mattresses on the floor, a tin bucket, and a couple of thin blankets.

"The least they could have done is taken off this duct tape," June said, looking down dejectedly at her wrists. She twisted her hands and pumped her fingers back and forth to keep the circulation going.

Adriana was already thinking about how to get the tape off her wrists. It was part of the plan her mind was busy formulating, a plan to escape.

# 13

TIRANA

"What do you think they're going to do to us?" June asked. She was expecting the worst despite what Tosu had told them. It was only a matter of time until the boss retired for the night, leaving the two women in an underground prison cell with hundreds of hormone-driven men who probably hadn't seen a woman in a long time.

Adriana didn't say it, but she had the feeling that June had never been in this kind of situation before. For Adriana, it was far from the first time, and she had a feeling it wouldn't be the last.

"Don't worry," she said.

"Don't worry?" June sounded exasperated. "We're locked in this cell with no way out. And even if we could find a way out, they took our guns and all our gear. We're screwed, Addy."

Adriana let her friend vent and then waited another ten seconds before she said anything. "You done?"

June's eyebrows lowered to reflect her frown. "What?"

"I have a plan."

"Plan? What plan? There is no plan! Our hands are literally tied here." June held up her hands to show the duct tape still binding them. She wrestled her arms around in another desperate attempt to get free of the bonds, but it was no use.

Adriana just flashed a crooked grin and stepped over to the tin bucket sitting on the floor. The thing was stained on the inside and smelled like a porta potty that hadn't been cleaned in a year.

She winced at the odor and choked back the impulse to vomit as she took a knee next to the receptacle. She reached out with her bound hands and pried a finger under the pail's wiry handle. It creaked as she lifted it. *Good, it's loose*, she thought. A quick inspection of where the handle was attached to the bucket revealed the loop had a small gap as it wrapped around to meet itself.

"That thing is disgusting," June said. "I hope you're not thinking of using it right now."

Adriana ignored her and pulled hard on one end of the handle, twisting it while she braced the edge with her foot. The tin bent easily under her leverage, and the gap in the handle's loop increased. She planted her foot back on the ground and checked her handiwork. Then she twisted the handle again and pulled the end through the hole on the bucket.

"What in the world are you doing?"

"Funny thing, duct tape," Adriana answered without looking up. She twisted the other end of the handle the same way she'd done the first and a moment later had removed the entire piece of metal from the pail. "It's extremely strong but very easy to tear."

She twisted the wiry handle around in her fingers. "Come here."

June wasn't sure what Adriana had in mind, and then it hit her. The handle's end had the slightest of edges to it. She hurried over to Adriana, who set to work scratching into the thick gray surface. It took less than a minute before there was a small cut on the bonds.

They would have simply torn the tape free with the end, but Tosu's men weren't stupid. They knew the women would think of that, so had wrapped the end of the duct tape inside where their wrists were and then mashed it down so it couldn't be peeled by prying fingers.

Three minutes passed before the cut was wide enough to peel

back. Once that was done, Adriana set the handle on the ground and used her fingernails to pry the tape away from the wrappings. One loop at a time, she unraveled the bindings until June's wrists were free.

Overwhelmed with relief, and blood flowing to her fingers gain, June repeated the process for Adriana, making quick work of the duct tape.

Adriana tossed the makeshift bindings on the floor and rubbed her wrists to get the feeling back.

"Okay, so we're free of those things," June said, "but we're still stuck."

Adriana flashed a mischievous grin. "I have a plan for that, too."

She moved over to the door and pounded on the surface with a fist. There was no response. She rapped on the door again, harder than before. The impact with the base of her hand hurt, but she didn't care.

"Hey, we need some help in here!" she shouted.

Still nothing.

She kicked the door this time, using her heel to keep the impact to her foot to a minimum. "You hear me out there? We need help with the bucket!"

June raised an eyebrow, imagining the images going through the minds of the guards who were stationed just outside the door.

At that moment, the sound of the lock releasing clicked through the metal barrier and Adriana put her hands behind her back. They'd wonder how she'd gotten free of the duct tape if they saw her wrists. She was banking on them not realizing her hands were behind instead of in front of her until it was too late.

The door swung open, and the two guards stepped in. One had a submachine gun pointed at Adriana. The other held a pistol out in front of him. These guys were taking no chances.

"What is the problem?" the first guard asked, lowering his weapon slightly. The muzzle was pointed right at Adriana's abdomen.

"The bucket," Adriana said. "We can't use the bathroom with our hands tied like this."

The guard frowned and stepped farther into the room. He lowered his pistol while the other guy stood in the doorway with his gun still pointing menacingly at Adriana. The first guy turned his head to see what she was talking about.

June was standing near the wall with her hands behind her back. She offered a sheepish grin. "Sorry," she said. "I really gotta pee."

The guard shook his head and started to move toward her when he felt something grab his left wrist. He tried to spin around to face the threat, but Adriana was counting on that. She used his momentum to turn him in a 180 degree arc until he was facing his comrade. Then she jumped on his back and wrapped her forearm around his thick neck, and squeezed.

The second guard moved his weapon around but couldn't get a clear shot.

June saw both men were preoccupied and grabbed the bucket off the floor. She flung it at the guy in the doorway, striking him in the temple.

Stunned but not knocked out, he slumped against the doorframe, rubbing the side of his head.

It was all the time June needed. She flew across the room like a banshee.

The man saw her coming, but there was nothing he could do. He raised his weapon to fire, but June leaped into the air and plowed the heel of her boot into the same place on his head the bucket had struck a moment before. The other side of his head smashed into the rock wall, and he fell limp to the floor.

Meanwhile, Adriana was having the bull ride of her life. The first guard spun around in circles, desperately swinging his arms to free himself of the parasite. He saw his partner go down in one kick from the other prisoner and tried to lift his gun to end her life right then and there. Adriana saw what he was doing and wrapped the fingers of her other hand around his face, digging her nails deep into his eyes.

He howled in pain one second. The next, his pistol dropped to the floor with a clack.

Adriana squeezed harder with her forearm, closing off the man's airway. June grabbed the submachine gun and stepped back away from the door, closing it quickly so no one would notice the struggle within.

The first guard dropped to his knees, eyes bulging from their sockets. His face flushed as the air he so badly needed was kept from entering his body.

June watched with her new weapon trained on the man's chest. If he managed to wriggle free, she'd shoot him dead, but that would raise alarms. She could see Adriana had it handled as the man slumped forward, prostrate on the floor.

Adriana let go and let his head smack on the ground. She checked his pulse and found none, but that didn't satisfy her.

She reached down to his belt and took a tactical knife with a black handle out of a sheath, and shoved the tip unceremoniously into the base of his skull. Then she moved over and did the same to the second guard.

June's forehead wrinkled as she watched her partner ruthlessly make certain the men were dead. She'd never seen someone do anything like that. Killing? Absolutely. It was what her line of work called for sometimes. But Adriana may as well have been a high school biology student cutting open frogs or fish. The ease with which she killed was almost clinical.

Adriana wiped the blade on the second guard's shirt and then tucked it in her belt on her right hip.

"Was that...um...you know what, never mind," June said. She was going to ask if that was necessary then thought better of it. Making sure a bad guy was dead wasn't a terrible idea at this point. Getting shot in the back *was*.

Adriana picked up the pistol from the ground and checked to make sure it would fire.

She motioned to the door. "What do you say we get out of here?"

"It's gonna be tough," June said. "Lot of guys between us and the exit."

"Then we take them all out, along with their weapons. We can't leave this place standing."

June let a grin creep across her face. Her friend was more ruthless than she anticipated, and it was exactly what they needed.

"Let's take 'em down, then," June said.

# 14

TIRANA

Adriana stepped out of the cell and scanned the room. June joined her on the other side of the door, analyzing the other side of the huge chamber.

Most of the men in the area were still busily working on assembling weapons or ammunition. They hadn't been noticed yet.

Both women knew they were on borrowed time before an alarm went off. They'd have to move with speed and precision to eliminate as many enemies as possible. Catching them off guard was key. The women were outnumbered, but those odds would improve with every terrorist life they took.

Adriana spotted a guy to her right patrolling the area with his submachine gun hanging casually from his shoulder. He had one finger by the trigger but was unaware an escape was happening right under his nose.

Adriana motioned for June to slip back into the cell and then closed the door, leaving it slightly ajar. She watched the crack at the door's bottom until she saw the shadow of the man appear. He was probably wondering what happened to the two guards.

She had intentionally left the door opened ever so slightly so he would see it. Then curiosity would get the better of him.

Just as she hoped, the door pushed open and the man stepped in with his HK-5 held waist high. He saw June standing to the right with a sheepish smile on her face. Her weapon was behind her back. The next second, he saw the two dead men on the floor.

Immediately, his eyes widened, and he reached for the radio on his jacket. Adriana pounced from behind, driving her weapon through the guy's neck and out the front just below the chin. He gurgled and fell to his knees but managed to fire one round from his weapon before Adriana wrenched the gun from his hands.

The bullet ricocheted around the room, bouncing off the rough walls until it dove into the floor and died.

Adriana picked up the guy's weapon and slung it over her shoulder. Nothing wrong with accumulating more guns.

She gave a nod to June, who rushed back to the door and poked her head around. No one saw what had happened, the noise outside thankfully masking the sound of the shot fired.

They still had the element of surprise, and it was time to use it.

She and Adriana crept out of the cell and skirted along the wall to the left behind a stack of wooden crates. The huge boxes were marked with Russian words. Both women knew what they said, but there was no doubt the phrases and letters were to throw off any casual observer who took a gander, claiming the contents were parts for household appliances.

They stayed behind the crates for a moment, assessing the situation. Every man in the room was armed. Most of them had the same submachine guns June and Adriana now carried. Some had pistols; still others had Kalashnikovs. Those were the ones that could deal serious damage. AK-47s were the weapon of choice for most terrorist groups. They were cheap enough to get if the Chinese versions were available, though those were prone to jamming and breaking more easily than the Russian ones. In the years since the fall of communism, the Russian models were more readily available on the black market.

Either way, the rounds from those guns were devastating, capable of blowing off a limb if placed correctly. The weapons were difficult to control, though, and had serious kickback from each shot, making firing them on full auto fairly problematic.

Then there was the noise factor to consider. Blasts from the AKs in this enclosed environment would be deafening. Most gunfire would. June and Adriana didn't have the luxury of worrying about the long-term effects of a gunfight on their hearing. They had to take down this facility. It was the only thing that mattered.

To their immediate left, two men were busily assembling the lower receivers to a collection of guns. Adriana motioned with her eyes and a flick of the head that they should take out those two first, although it would expose them to the rest of the guys in the room, which she counted at twenty-seven.

Between the two of them, she knew they had at least that many rounds, but there was no way they'd hit the mark on every shot. Extras were always welcome. Fortunately, with every target they took down, they'd receive a fresh complement of bullets.

"I'll take out those two," Adriana said, turning to her friend. She spoke in whispers that were little more than breaths passing through her lips. "When I do, the rest of the men will come my way. My guess is they will hesitate to fire initially. They don't want a bunch of bullets flying around in this place." Her eyes played around the room for a second before returning to June. "Take out the men with the AKs first. Then we target the rest, eliminate the closest, and go from there."

June gave a reluctant nod. She didn't like the idea of Adriana stepping out of cover to take out the two men at the table to their left, but she also knew it was a good plan. As the commander of the mission, she should have volunteered to take the lead. The determination on Adriana's face shut down that notion before it even popped up.

"Ready?" Adriana asked.

June swallowed. She didn't let on, but the butterflies in her stomach felt more like hornets after a run-in with a bear. Her nerves had always been a problem, and in situations like this she told herself her anxiety kept her sharp, alert to every possible threat. So far, it seemed to be working. She'd managed to survive several close calls during assaults not dissimilar to the one they were about to begin. She hoped her good fortune would continue.

"Let's go," she said.

Adriana gave a nod and then stood up from her position and stalked toward the two men at the work table. The one to the left noticed her first, catching movement out of the corner of his eye.

When Adriana began her approach, they were only thirty feet away. When the guy turned to look at her, the gap was twenty. He was caught off guard when he laid eyes on her, apparently assuming the movement was coming from one of the guards or another worker. His eyes widened, then narrowed, and he reached for the gun hanging by his hip.

She was already holding the tip of her knife in her right hand when the guy went for his weapon. Adriana kept walking straight at him, barely tweaking her upper body as she reached back and flung the blade at the man.

The sharp tip plunged into his left eye. He yelped and collapsed in a heap at his colleague's feet. The second guy reacted faster, shouting at the approaching woman as she raised her pistol and squeezed the trigger.

The muzzle erupted in a flash. The bullet found its mark on the right side of the man's forehead and dropped him to the ground.

The gunshots thundered in the underground facility. The sound echoed around the big room and down through the tunnel leading to the exit. Adriana knew what was coming next. She twisted to the right as the rest of the bad guys in the room looked in her direction. She pointed the pistol at the next target and dropped him instantly. The second guy was starting to react but still too slowly. He caught two rounds in the chest. A third was too close to number two and made for an easy shot. Finally, one of the terrorists put up a fight, spun around, and raised his weapon in time to be struck with three rounds from Adriana's weapon.

Shouting ensued. Adriana saw several men running her way with guns raised. They were yelling in Arabic along with a few minor dialects, but it was difficult to understand what they were saying. Not that it mattered. She figured they were telling her to put down her gun or something.

They never knew what hit them.

June popped up from behind the crates to the right and opened fire. She sprayed metal at the onrushing men, knocking down those with the Kalashnikovs in the first few seconds. The onslaught continued, bullets tearing through the enemy ranks with ease, dropping them one by one from the flank.

The remaining terrorists tried to recover. They skidded to a stop and whirled to their left to address the new shooter, but that left them well within Adriana's range.

Only two of the men bothered to stay focused on her, which did them little good. Adriana flung the submachine gun around while June ducked for cover.

Adriana strode forward with the automatic weapon at her hip, spitting death at the terrorists. The only two guys looking at her were the first casualties of her renewed assault. One took a round each to the thigh, abdomen, and heart. The second was less fortunate, receiving a bullet in the groin that rendered him useless.

The overwhelming advantage the terrorists once had was, in mere seconds, whittled down to almost nothing. The remaining eight guys scattered for cover as Adriana continued the onslaught.

June remained crouched out of sight while Adriana ripped their ranks apart, giving June enough of a reprieve to grab another weapon from one of the fallen bad guys.

The last four terrorists scattered and ran. June shot one in the back as he tried to escape back toward the main exit. The other three managed to dive for cover. Two of them stayed together behind a row of pallets and boxes while the third found a stack of metal cylinders.

Adriana picked up two more submachine guns from the ground and held them at her hips. June stood up from her position and scanned the room. One of the terrorists saw her head pop up and fired. The round narrowly missed, hitting the crate to her left just a foot away. The wood splintered as she dropped back down for a moment.

The two men were still flanked by Adriana, though not exposed as they'd been before. The man closest to her peeked around the corner of the pallets and received a bullet into the wood near his face. He jumped back to safety and waited.

Adriana fired one more shot to make it look like she was pressing the brute force attack, then hurried over on tiptoe to stay silent, ducking behind a forklift. The terrorist nearest the exit raised his head and fired at June's position, and then dropped out of sight again.

Now they were in a stalemate.

Adriana stole a look around the room, keeping behind the forklift's bulky lower frame. There wasn't much to work with. Cables ran along the rocks above the two men positioned together. There were dozens of lights in the room, so shooting them out wouldn't work. And there was no sign of a fuse box to kill the power. Of course there wasn't. That kind of thing would be up at the main building.

There had to be something she could use.

June popped up and fired two rounds at the metal cylinders. The bullets ricocheted in bright yellow sparks off the gray metal. She knew hitting the target would be nearly impossible. The guy wasn't giving her anything. June knew she had to let him know that she'd do the same.

Adriana sighed, frustrated. She needed a way to draw the men out of their cover. Then it hit her.

She looked up at the forklift's seat and craned her neck enough to spot the keys dangling from the ignition. Two huge boxes sat on a pallet already snagged by the heavy steel forks.

*Really?*

She'd take it.

Adriana poked her head around the machine and fired four warning shots at the men behind the pallets. They kicked their feet and pressed their backs harder against the stacks of wood, desperate not to get hit.

A second after firing, Adriana hopped into the forklift and turned the key.

The propane-driven machine grumbled to life. She flipped a

switch and then pulled on a lever. The fork started rising from the ground, putting the boxes on the front between her and the two terrorists.

Adriana spun the wheel and then stepped on the accelerator.

The forklift's motor groaned, and it lurched forward. The boxes shifted slightly but stayed on top of the pallet as she guided it straight toward the two hiding terrorists.

The men heard the machine's engine. They hesitated for a second, not knowing what they should do. One of them had had enough. He popped up and opened fire, spraying the contents of his magazine at the oncoming threat. The other guy jumped from cover and made a run for the exit.

June saw movement around the corner of her crates. "Where you going?" she said to herself. She aimed the HK-5 and squeezed off four quick rounds, one at a time.

One of the rounds struck the man in the side and knocked him over. He writhed in agony, clutching at the wound. June fired another shot into his chest, and he stopped moving, save for a death twitch.

Adriana kept her foot on the gas, pushing the forklift forward. The gunman's magazine ran dry and he reached for his sidearm as he stumbled backward.

June saw her man peek out from behind the cylinders at the moving machine. He fired a shot that pinged off the forklift's metal body. June didn't hesitate. The guy would have an angle on Adriana the second she plowed the big machine into the stacks of pallets. June sprinted from her position to the other end of the cylinders and squatted down. She looked down the length of the tubes and saw the man, stuck her weapon into the opening, and fired.

Bullets sparked off the inside of the cylinder, delivering a deafening and deadly blizzard of rounds.

The terrorist never knew what hit him. The bullets tore into him, and he fell over onto his side.

Adriana risked a short peek down under the boxes ahead of her and saw the row of crates approaching. The lone gunman was firing one shot at a time with his pistol, hoping to squeeze a bullet through an opening and hit the driver. A second before the forklift rammed into the pallets, Adriana jumped to the right and rolled on the ground. She stayed low to remain unseen even as the big machine hit the stack with a thunderous crash. Boxes tumbled to the ground. Wood fractured and splintered. The forklift lost its momentum and ground to a halt, but the shooter was still focused on it as he backed away toward the exit.

Adriana used his confusion. Keeping low to the floor, she crept around the wreckage, working her way between the terrorist and the tunnel to freedom.

The man fired his pistol again and again. His hand trembled, and he wore a terrified look on his face. He never saw the brunette woman sneak up behind him.

Adriana pressed her weapon's hot muzzle to the back of the gunman's skull. "Put it down," she ordered.

He started and was about to turn around out of sheer instinct.

"Don't," she said.

He froze.

"Put the gun down." She didn't know if he spoke English or not. All of the men looked different. The Red Ring wasn't being exclusive with its recruitment. This guy was probably from the Balkans based on his appearance.

He held his weapon out and lowered it to the ground, and then raised up with his hands in the air.

"Very good," she said and spun him around by the shoulder.

June trotted up, sweeping the area with her weapon to make sure the room was clear. Bodies were strewn all over the place. Most were piled in the center of the floor where they'd been clustered together, making for the easiest targets. June wiped a bead of sweat from her forehead with the back of her hand.

"Now," Adriana said to the man, staring into his fear-filled eyes, "where is Tosu?"

# 15

TIRANA

Tosu slid into a comfortable chair and lit a cigar. His plan had worked perfectly, and the two heathens were now locked up in the mine, surrounded by more than two dozen of his holy soldiers.

He sucked a puff of smoke into his mouth and held it for a moment before blowing it back out. The little office was set up on the side of the mining camp's main building. It was nothing more than a trailer that had been converted into a foreman's workstation, but it served its purpose on rare occasions such as this.

Tosu almost never visited the facility unless it was to oversee some critical aspect of their operation. That tended to be during testing or to give an assignment to one of the lieutenants.

He purposely hadn't taken the two women to the other parts of the mine where the men were being trained. The sight of them might have incited a riot. Some of them hadn't seen a woman in months, only setting foot outside for training exercises and fresh air.

He took another puff of the smoke. While he professed a righteous disposition to the men under his command, deep down he secretly coveted the two women for himself. They would make a fine addition to his harem, though he knew that would never be possible.

They were too dangerous to keep alive. He had no idea who they were, but there was no denying their lethal capabilities. He'd set the trap with the knowledge that Qufar Abdi had given up as much as he probably could. While Qufar had proved himself useful over and over again, and loyal to the cause, Tosu also knew the man was weak, easily broken if the right pressure was applied.

Tosu had hoped—for a fairly long time—that Qufar would come around and embrace the true spirit of their movement. That's what it was, after all: a revolution against the greed of the West, a desperate cry by a holy few to right the planet and turn it into a sanctuary Allah would be proud of.

But that conversion had never truly happened for Qufar. It was better to kill him and let him get his reward a little early rather than have him suffer at the hands of the nonbelievers.

The phone rang in Tosu's pocket, and he pulled it out. He didn't have to look at the screen to know who it was. He'd requested the Teacher to call him at this exact time, and the older man was never late. Punctuality, he said, was honorable.

"It is done," Tosu said two seconds after hitting the green button on his device. "The heathen women are in the mine now with no way to escape."

"Good," the gravelly voice said. "You have done well, my Son. I knew you would not fail me."

"Of course not."

There was a long pause, and for a second Tosu wondered if the call had dropped. He looked at the screen and noted two bars in the display's top corner. Nope. The call was still live.

"I wonder, though," the old man said, "why you didn't execute the nonbelievers on sight."

Tosu had anticipated this question before putting the entire plan together. His trap had worked to perfection. Knowing the women and their allies would try to find him, Tosu set about sending fake signals on the dark web. He knew if he put out too many breadcrumbs, they would sense trouble and immediately become suspicious. So he only put two offers out there, and in two different parts of the world.

He assumed whoever the women worked for would have a dossier on him, some kind of file that gave away his personal information, including his country of origin. It was how surveillance operated. And while he wasn't sure which group had come after him, he knew they all thought the same way, with many similar protocols in place.

It was only natural, then, that when they found the offer to buy weapons on the dark web from a buyer in Albania, the women would follow the trail all the way to his front door.

He'd decided before they ever entered his city that he wasn't going to kill them right away. They would suffer by watching the wretched masses burn.

"I felt it prudent," Tosu said, answering the older man's question. "I like to have bargaining chips just in case. And besides, they should be made to suffer for their sins. They will watch the attacks unfold with no chance of being able to help."

There was another moment of silence. "Very well, Khalil. I trust your judgment on this matter. You have not failed me before."

"Thank you."

"Now, how are things progressing? Are we on schedule?"

Tosu knew that would be the man's next question. "No, sir." He let his answer hang for a second before he added, "We're ahead of schedule. Our preparations will be finished within the next forty-eight hours. Then you may proceed as planned."

The old man couldn't hide the surprise in his voice. "Excellent."

"I'll let the others know that their shipments should arrive by the first of next week. Then the nonbelievers will see the true glory of our cause."

"Indeed."

Tosu knew who the others were, though he'd only met them once. They were all leaders of the Red Ring, strategically placed in eight locales throughout the world. Each location was a major population center—and a target—but each was more than that. One cell was in Chicago, another in New York, London, Paris, Tokyo, Sydney, and Mumbai.

The strikes would come simultaneously and without warning. First, the rockets would hit the city centers. Thousands would die immediately from the explosions. Then the bioweapons would kick in. Tens of thousands would be infected with the illness. The afflicted nations would rally their doctors and hospitals, but with such an outbreak there would be no way to mass produce the cure fast enough.

Some could be saved, but in the end the disease would be overwhelming.

And then there was the matter of the eighth cell.

They were positioned in Atlanta, ready to take out the Centers for Disease Control. The facility was one of the most heavily fortified in the world. It was the Fort Knox of biological research. But it had weaknesses just like any other government operation.

So the most powerful bombs would be delivered there. But they wouldn't be sent via rocket. The Teacher had selected a group of brave men who were ready to die for the cause. They would enter the building one at a time. The first would go in with guns blazing. The second would detonate a device strapped to his chest. With the walls broken and the entrance wide open, the third and fourth men would charge ahead and finish the job, detonating two powerful explosives within the compound.

With the CDC out of the way, America's and its allies' fight against the biowar would be severely hindered. Millions would die within the first month. Governments would fall. People would stay in their homes. The world would sink to its knees.

Tosu believed in what they were doing. He knew that nothing like this had ever been attempted before. He likened it to the Spartans fighting the Persians in the Battle of Thermopylae where only three hundred soldiers were able to fight off enemies numbering in the tens of thousands.

This, however, wasn't a defensive play. It was an attack. The Red Ring was only two thousand in number, but put in the right places they could wreak havoc.

Unsuspecting civilians would be helpless. The police and military would be too slow to react, and by the time they did the Red Ring's men would disappear, ready to attack another target when the command was given.

The targets had been chosen with great care, in places where guns weren't permitted. Tosu and his master would have loved nothing more than to strike places like Dallas or Houston, but the Southern United States was a crapshoot. In that region, more citizens were armed than not. While many infidels would die, so would many of the Red Ring's soldiers.

Not that that mattered. They were going to likely die anyway, either from combat or from the disease that would spread. Either way, they'd intentionally left out that part of the United States. Those people would be taken care of by the biological weapons.

"Carry on," the Teacher said, interrupting Tosu's thoughts. "I will prepare a speech to share with our legions. Let me know when all the preparations have been made."

"I will."

Tosu ended the call and took another drag on his cigar. Everything was falling into place.

That thought was the last thing to run through his mind a second before the alarms started sounding.

He sat up in his chair. "What? What is going on?"

He grabbed a phone on the desk and picked it up, punching several buttons before putting the receiver to his ear. The line was dead.

Tosu slammed the phone down and hurried out of the room, leaving the cigar smoldering in an ashtray.

He ran back into the main building, down a corridor to the security room where he knew two of his men were monitoring the facility with a series of displays. Tosu burst through the door and found chaos inside. The two men were shouting orders into their headsets. On one of the screens, Tosu saw the carnage in the room outside the cell where he'd put the women. His men were lying all over the place, a few of them heaped onto one another.

"What is going on?" he demanded anew. Then he saw movement

on another screen. The blonde woman was firing her weapon as the brunette moved up through the tunnel. Two more of his men fell.

"The prisoners, sir," one of the men said, "they—"

His comment was cut off by gunshots coming from just outside the building.

The women were almost there.

A million questions ran through Tosu's mind. The biggest of all was how had the women managed to escape. It should have been impossible. They were locked up, surrounded, with no hope to get away. Yet here they were, knocking on his door.

"Sir, we have another problem," one of the security guys said in his thick Serbian accent.

"What?"

The security guy pointed at the image of the main room. A stack of crates had been opened, revealing explosives within. Rockets were close by as well as piles of other munitions. One of Tosu's men was tied to one of the wooden boxes, wrapped tight with wiring.

Tosu could see the fear in his eyes. The guy was looking straight into the camera and then motioning to the bombs directly behind him.

"No," Tosu said.

The word had barely escaped his lips when the entire mountain shuddered. Most of the cameras on the wall flashed static and then went blank. The old metal facility rocked and trembled.

He took a deep breath through his nose and exhaled with disbelief. In a matter of minutes, he'd gone from the cause's hero to losing everything. Their guns, explosives, bioweapons...everything was gone, destroyed in the explosion and the resulting collapse of the mine tunnels.

The shock blurred his vision. He felt his body waver. How could this have happened? The question kept coming back along with another thought: *I have to get out of here.*

"Get to the trucks," he ordered.

Tosu spun around and rushed out the door.

# 16

TIRANA

Adriana saw Tosu first as he busted out of the building, running down the gravel road toward the SUVs parked at the bottom.

"Sweep the building," Adriana said. "I got Tosu."

June looked at her friend. She didn't argue. She could see Adriana's mind was made up and there would be no changing it. She gave a nod and ran off toward the doors the man had just come through.

Adriana bolted ahead, racing after the terrorist. Her feet pounded the gravel, kicking up loose rocks behind her.

Tosu caught a glimpse of her out of the corner of his eye and raised his pistol. He fired the Desert Eagle four times, wildly missing but doing enough to cause Adriana to duck and weave, slowing her down as he made his way down the hill.

The second he turned his attention away from her, she steadied the submachine gun and pushed forward. Her finger squeezed the trigger. The muzzle popped over and over again. She tried to keep Tosu in her sights, but the weapon wasn't made for ranges like this.

The gun clicked, and she tossed it aside. She reached back and grabbed a pistol out of her belt. She'd taken the weapon on her way out of the building. Now it was all she had.

Adriana pumped her legs harder now. Her heels kicked up high as she descended the hill. Tosu was nearly to the first SUV. He skidded to a stop and fumbled with the keys.

She wasn't close enough to be accurate but definitely close enough to scare the guy. She raised the pistol as the gap closed five feet at a time. Adriana fired. The bullet smashed into the back-left window and shattered it.

The sudden explosion of glass and the sound of gunfire behind him spooked Tosu. He fiddled with the keys one more time, but another shot plunking into the SUV's driver-side door startled him and he dropped them onto the gravel.

He spun around with his weapon raised and fired five wild shots at the onrushing woman.

Adriana dove behind some big rocks to her left and waited, took several breaths, and then poked her head around the stone, pistol in front of her face.

She had the SUV in her sights but no sign of Tosu.

She swallowed and crept out of her hiding spot, still ready for a sudden attack.

Her eyes panned the area. The hill to the right swept up the mountainside. A few outcroppings of large rocks dotted the slope, but Tosu wouldn't have had time to get there.

Adriana knew there were only two places he could go: down the hill or hiding out and lying in wait.

She moved deftly along the driveway, keeping to the hard dirt off the path for extra stealth. Gravel was loose, and the weight of her boots would cause it to crunch and move. Maybe Tosu wouldn't hear; maybe he would. It was a risk she didn't want to take.

Reaching the bend in the driveway where the little parking area curved in, she paused and looked around. No sign of Tosu. Adriana bent down and looked under the chassis of the SUVs, thinking he was probably hiding behind one. Still nothing. She frowned. Had the man taken off down the road?

Her question was answered with several loud bangs. Tosu popped up from just behind a drop-off where the parking lot ended and the stony ground began.

Adriana dove for cover, rolling to a stop a few dozen feet behind the nearest vehicle. She clambered up and scurried over to the back bumper and waited, keeping her feet as narrow of a target as possible as she hid behind the back-left tire.

Knowing that to stay still would be a death sentence, she risked a step around to her left and peeked around the corner. Tosu was gone again.

Adriana skipped over to the next SUV and waited for a few seconds, then repeated the move to the last one in the row. She kept close to the vehicle's body, her back pressed against it as she shuffled around to the passenger side. Her pistol was held close to her chin, ready to turn and fire at a second's notice.

She was betting on Tosu still being in his place, waiting to pop up again to fire. By looping around, Adriana hoped to flank him and take him down safely from the side.

She kept creeping forward until she reached the front of the SUV. There, she paused another moment and leaned around the bumper. She swept the gun barrel right and then left but found no trace of the man in her sights.

She was about to step out and rush down the hill when she heard a noise behind her.

Adriana swirled around, but it was too late. Tosu was standing over her with his gun pointed at her head.

"Don't...move," he said in an even tone. But his face trembled. And his eyes overflowed with fear—not of her but of a greater fate, one he would now be running from for the rest of his life.

Adriana was only halfway turned around when he gave the order. She froze in place and hesitated.

"Do it," he reiterated and flicked his pistol for extra menace.

"You lost," she said as she let the pistol drop to the ground. "You lost everything."

He flashed a yellow-toothed grin, cocking his head to the side.

Tosu had the look of a crazy man now, a guy with nothing to lose because he'd just watched his life's work destroyed right before his eyes.

He gave a faint nod. "Yes. So it would seem. But I can still kill you. At least I have that satisfaction."

"The Red Ring won't tolerate this failure," she said, trying to keep him talking. "You'll be hunted down like a dog, probably tortured before they finally give you the mercy of death."

"Perhaps. But there will be one less infidel around."

He squeezed the trigger. The weapon clicked.

Tosu's eyes widened.

He pulled the trigger again. Same result.

Adriana didn't wait for a third time. She sprang at the man, driving her shoulder into his midsection as she pumped her legs.

Tosu's heel caught the ground and he fell backward. His head hit the loose rocks and sent his vision into a spin. His head throbbed all of a sudden. He swung his arms around and kicked his legs, desperately trying to get the woman off him.

Adriana squeezed her knees together, crushing his ribs as she drove fist after fist into the man's face. Her arms weakened with every blow, so she turned to hammer blows to finish the fight, driving the bridge of one hand then the other into his nose and jaw.

Finally, when her energy was gone and Tosu's head looked like a swollen skin piñata, she pushed herself off him and stood. Her breaths came fast and hard.

She staggered backward until she found the pistol she'd dropped a minute before, bent down and picked it up, then made her way back over to the beaten man.

He looked up at her with swollen eyes. A gash oozed blood under his left. More crimson trickled from his broken nose.

"Now you're going to talk," she said, pointing the gun at his right knee.

He snorted a laugh, which shot more blood from his nostrils. Then his bleeding lips parted, showing off a missing tooth from the bottom row. His head twisted back and forth. "I'm not telling you anything," he said. "You don't understand. You and all the other nonbelievers will soon be gone. And there's nothing you can do to stop it. My place in paradise is assured."

Adriana pinched her eyebrows together, wrinkling her forehead. *What was he talking about?* They'd just taken out an arsenal of weapons. While he may not have intended to, Tosu had just divulged a useful bit of information. That told her he knew more.

"Maybe you won't talk," she said, "but we'll certainly make the rest of your life extremely uncomfortable."

He shook his head. "No. I'm already dead."

His smile widened, and she could see the white foam through his yellow teeth. Tosu's body started shaking violently as the poison entered his blood. His eyes were wide with fear and agony. The toxins did their work fast, burning into his organs with extraordinary speed.

"No," Adriana said with a sense of urgency in her voice. "No!"

She bent down and grabbed the dying man by the shoulders. "Tell me what you're talking about!"

The only thing she got in return was a desperate look of pain on Tosu's face before his eyes fixed on a place in the sky. He was gone.

She let his head drop back to the gravel. Adriana cursed herself for not realizing what the man might do. There was no way to know he'd kill himself. Was there?

After a quick check of Tosu's neck and finding no pulse, she made her way back up the driveway. June might still need her help. She picked up the pace, moving at a jog, which was all she could muster at that point.

She held her weapon at the ready and pushed through the door to the main building. June was standing just inside. She was hovering over two men. One was lying facedown on the floor with a trail of blood coming from his chest. The other was on his knees with hands in the air.

"You get Tosu?" June asked without looking over her shoulder. It was like she knew Adriana won the fight without seeing it.

"Yeah, but he's dead," Adriana answered. "Took cyanide, I think."

June cocked her head to the side and stared at her prisoner. "You're not gonna do that, are you?"

The frightened man shook his head vehemently.

"Good," Adriana said, "because I have some questions for you."

# 17

LONDON

"**B**reaking news out of Albania," a news anchor said. "Allied forces struck a major blow to a terrorist group located just outside the Albanian capital of Tirana yesterday."

The television displayed the destroyed mine and the building outside it.

"No word yet on how many casualties were involved in the strike, but sources say at least twenty terrorists were taken out."

Adriana looked up from her tea with a raised eyebrow. *Twenty?* She rolled her eyes. She wished it had only been twenty.

The screen cut away to the White House press secretary. "The attack was carried out by two of our bombers based in Germany," the man said.

He continued rambling on about the types of weapons used, the planes involved, and a bunch of other lies the American government spun.

Adriana didn't judge. She knew why President Dawkins had to mislead the public. If people knew what was really going on, there could be major upheaval. Best to keep the common folk in the dark about certain things.

Of course, Dawkins hadn't even known about the mission until it was already done.

June had apprised him of the situation and given him the story to share with the media based on what Shadow Cell's director suggested.

Adriana took a sip of tea as the news outlet switched to sports. The guy on the screen was talking about the English men's national football team and their upcoming slate of games to get ready for the World Cup.

Her thoughts drifted to the next mission. She didn't even know what was coming next. Tosu was dead, an unfortunate casualty considering he knew more about Red Ring's operation than most of the others on their hit list. His death, however, was a warning to the rest of the terrorist organization that someone knew who they were, and that they were coming to take out the trash.

She reflected on the swift and brutal shootout in the mine. There was no guilt in her heart about the men she'd killed. They were bad people, ready to kill the innocent at a moment's notice, and themselves if necessary. Adriana had helped eliminate someone who could have dealt massive damage to the free world.

They'd left him on the gravel of the parking lot. He would serve as a warning to those who would consider that life, the life of bringing war to the innocent.

Adriana knew that whoever was in charge of Red Ring wouldn't be foolish enough to travel to the mine to inspect what happened. There would be authorities crawling all over the place for months, investigating the blast area along with anything else they could find.

The investigators, of course, didn't know what really happened. The Albanian officials had been slapped with an empty threat about harboring terrorists within their borders. Their leaders, confused and probably unaware, would put new policies in place that in the end would do little to stem the flow of extremists into their land.

For most nations, border protection was a constant problem. With countries that were far more passive about it, they may as well have not had any borders at all. In the case of Albania, a massive terrorist operation was going on right under the noses of their government, and yet they had done nothing to stop it.

The American president had issued a similar warning to Pakistan when Osama bin Laden was found and summarily eliminated there. The undertone of the warning was always the same: harbor terrorists, and you will have to deal with us.

Now it wasn't the United States coming into someone else's backyard. It was an agency shrouded in secrecy, operating from the shadows. The Red Ring would see what happened in Tirana. A twinge of doubt, maybe even fear, would creep into the minds of the men in charge.

Governments had to play by rules. There were certain things they could and could not do. Shadow Cell operated outside those boundaries, pushing the envelope.

Adriana considered that thought as she took another sip of tea. She and June had slaughtered every terrorist in the facility outside of Tirana. They'd cut them down like they were lower than animals.

The truth was they were exactly that. Those men she and June killed were preparing to murder thousands of innocent people. Maybe more. If it came down to a mother and her child or a guy with an AK-47 going on a rampage, it would be the gunman every single time.

Adriana had heard stories about people who dwelled on the faces of the people they'd killed in that line of work. Some cops had trouble getting over having to shoot a suspect in the line of duty despite the fact they had no other choice.

Adriana didn't feel like that at all, and it made her wonder if there was something wrong with her.

That night, after getting back from Albania, she slept as if nothing had happened. The only thought that woke her now and then was the curiosity tugging at her as to the whereabouts of the men in charge of the Red Ring.

She'd spoken to Sean that night on the phone. It had been a week since they'd had a chance to chat. He was off chasing down a lost relic or something. She knew Tommy was probably close by. When he'd asked what she was up to, Adriana wasn't sure how to respond. She'd never lied to him, and knew she never would when it came to matters of a personal nature. In this case, however, she didn't have a choice. She knew he wouldn't approve of her activities. He'd warn her, tell her that there were other people who could do that job.

Heck, there *were* other people doing that job.

Ironically, he was the one person in the world that should understand why she was doing it, why she was hunting down terrorists.

She could also see his side, though, and knew if he'd gone back to working for the secretive Axis agency, her feelings would be similar.

Adriana got through it by telling herself it was only temporary, that she wouldn't do this forever. Just long enough to eliminate the Red Ring and restore some semblance of safety to the free world.

Then another thought crept into her mind. What if that never happened?

She shook it off and went back to the story she'd given Sean. It was the second time she'd had to tell him a tall tale about her travels and what she was up to. He bought it, of course, because why wouldn't he? Sean had no reason not to trust her.

The door to the tea shop swung open and let in a burst of cold air from outside. June tapped her feet on the doormat to get rid of the snow on her boots before stepping inside.

She eased into a seat across from Adriana and set a stack of files on the table.

"What's that?" Adriana asked, taking another swig from her cup. She set the container down on a saucer. The porcelain clinked when it touched. The tea room was old-fashioned, rumored to date back to the 1700s. Adriana figured the interior decor certainly reflected that period. "Dossiers for terrorists?"

"Something like that," June said with a smile. "Although not necessarily the ones we're looking for."

"The prisoners give you what you wanted?"

"Sort of," June said with a shrug. "They gave us names, places, pickup times, even a few targets, but I get the feeling those guys didn't know that much. It could take weeks to piece together the information they shared."

"Weeks?"

"Yeah. By then, who knows? The men in charge of their little operation could disappear. They'll go into hiding and only resurface when they think the heat has been turned down."

Adriana took a deep breath and exhaled. "So...what now?"

"Now? I'm going to visit my boyfriend; that's what now. I'm sure Sean would love to see you, too."

"Shouldn't we be working on finding the guys responsible for all this mess?"

"Our top analysts are on it. They can work on that stuff faster than we can. And like I said, it might take them weeks, maybe longer to find even one guy on the list those prisoners gave us. They'll be underground for a while."

Adriana wondered if she could expedite things with some of her connections in the grayer parts of society. She had plenty of friends in low places, though when she thought about it she realized that most of them weren't connected to terrorists, not that she knew of.

"Sean and Tommy are off searching for some ancient relic right now," Adriana said. "I'm not even sure how to get in contact with them."

"Another ancient relic?" June let out a laugh. "I wonder what they've gotten themselves into this time."

Adriana rolled her shoulders. "Not sure. Although I got the distinct impression Sean didn't give me the details because he was embarrassed."

June chuckled. "Embarrassed? Of what?"

"I don't know," Adriana said with a shake of the head. "Like he didn't want me to know what he was trying to find."

"J. Edgar Hoover's women's clothing?"

Adriana let out a laugh. She was Spanish but had been Americanized enough to have heard the stories of the FBI's infamous first director.

"I doubt that's what they were looking for. He said it was very old and very important."

June nodded. "It always is with those two." She picked up a menu and browsed through it. Seeing nothing that whetted her appetite, she set it back down. "I suppose if we really want to track them down we can. Those two tend to leave a trail of destruction in their wake."

"Indeed. I'll give Sean a call later today and see where they are. Maybe if they're in this part of the world we can meet up."

"Good idea. For now, just be ready. When the guys in charge of the Red Ring resurface, we need to be able to move at a moment's notice."

"Understood."

# 18

UZBEKISTAN

"Thank you for the information," the Teacher said.

The man standing in front of him wore a cut that stretched from his temple down to the corner of his mouth. He looked like he'd been through a war. A bruise on his forehead, the cut on his face, and grime from smoke, dirt, and grease streaked his skin.

"Yes, Master." The reply was simple and respectful.

"It is a miracle that you managed to survive the explosion as well as find a way to get away from the mine undetected."

The old man gazed at his pupil with narrow, analytical eyes. He was probing the subordinate, though he was fairly certain the younger man didn't realize it.

"Allah be praised," the man said.

His pale face was more so than normal.

"Have you had anything to eat or drink since the ordeal?"

The younger man shook his head. "I knew I needed to tell you as soon as I could. And I wanted to fast for my sins."

The Teacher gave a long, dramatic nod. "You were right to do so."

He stood up and hobbled over to the younger man, putting his arm around the visitor's shoulders. He steered him around, facing a balcony door on the far side of the sparsely decorated room. There were no pictures, no sofas, no fancy tables. Only a few wooden chairs, a desk that looked like it was made from reclaimed wood, and candles on top of it.

If an outsider were to see the place, they'd have sworn a minimalist lived there.

"I wonder," the Teacher said as he guided his pupil toward the door, "how it was you were able to escape."

The younger man turned his head to look at his master. He had a confused expression on his face, wondering why the Teacher would ask that of him.

The master clarified. "You've given me good information on the two women, although we knew about them before. They were responsible, we think, for the destruction of our rockets that were going to strike London. But I find it odd that all of our men died except for you. So, please, enlighten me as to how you managed to get away unharmed."

The younger man swallowed hard. He could tell the Teacher was pressing him for a specific answer. "I didn't run like a coward if that's what you're saying, sir. I swear it. I would die for our cause." The young man's Eastern European accent had a nervous quiver to it.

"Interesting," the Teacher said, "because here you are, standing in my home while your brothers are dead in a mountain somewhere in Albania."

The older man didn't look at his guest, instead staring out the door at the snow-covered peaks of the Chatkal Mountains. He flung open the door, letting in a burst of cold air that shook the young man to his bones.

The Teacher showed no signs of the cold affecting him, though the visitor assumed it chilled him just as much, if not more.

"Shouldn't we stay inside, Master? It's very cold out here."

The old man nodded but ushered his guest out onto the balcony with him. "Yes, I just want you to see something."

He stopped at the white stone railing and placed his left hand on top of it. He gazed out at the majestic mountain range, rising up above all else in the region. The two could make out the tiny figures of skiers and snowboarders sliding down the slopes of Chimgan Mountain in the distance.

"It's funny, don't you think?" the Teacher asked after a moment of reflection.

"What's that?" There was a quiver in the young man's voice.

"People spend so much time trying to enjoy this life, trying to cling to it with all their might, with every ounce of their being. They pray for more years or better health, when the truth is that the life that awaits us is far greater. Eternity will be spent in paradise for those of us who have been true to the word of mighty Allah."

The younger man nodded.

"Of course, for those who have betrayed the cause and put themselves and their own preservation before it, their eternal fate will be much different."

The young man frowned at the comment, immediately understanding that the Teacher was referring to his escape from Tirana.

"Master, I swear—"

The old man gripped the railing with one hand and the back of his guest's shirt with the other. His fingers were stronger than they appeared, as if imbued with some supernatural force. He used the rail for leverage and found it surprisingly easy to throw the younger man over. His terrified screams faded as he fell.

The Teacher watched the body tumbled through the air, four stories, until it struck the concrete driveway below with a sudden and terrible smack.

The old man turned away and walked back into his home as if the murder hadn't even happened. He knew someone else would clean up the mess. In fact, he'd already told his second in command what would happen. At that very moment, there were probably six or seven men rushing to dispose of the body and wash down the concrete.

The treasonous young man would be fed to the dogs, a fate he deserved for abandoning the others.

Sure, there was a flicker of doubt in the Teacher's mind. The man he'd just killed had given him as much information as he could. And the boy didn't have to come all the way to Uzbekistan. He'd done it of his own accord.

Had he decided to lie low for a while, maybe drop off the radar, he might still be alive.

It didn't matter in the grand scheme of things.

The men of the Red Ring had to know that failure was unacceptable, and that retreating was not an option.

"Aziz!" he shouted. His voice echoed through the chamber encased in sandstone.

A moment later, a man with a nearly bald head and dark, thick eyebrows walked through a door at the other end. He wore a gray peacoat and black pants. A pistol hung from a holster on the inside of his jacket.

"Yes, sir?" The guy stopped just a few feet into the room.

"How are preparations coming at our second installation?"

"The men are working as fast as they can, day and night. Some of them aren't even taking sleep. That facility will have everything ready on schedule."

"Good," the Teacher said. "I'm sure you're aware of what happened in Albania to our brothers there."

Aziz gave a somber nod but said nothing.

"That sets us back, but we can adapt. Our timeline will have to be pushed forward. Have that one and our third facility add more men. We have recruits waiting for orders, yes?"

"Yes," Aziz said and gave another nod.

"Reinforce both installations, and make sure that the men get at least a few hours of sleep and are well cared for. While I appreciate their fervor, the last thing we need is shoddy preparations. Everything must work perfectly, down to the guns they fire on the nonbelievers."

"Of course, sir. I will take care of it."

"You may leave."

Aziz nodded and left the room.

The Teacher eased back into his seat and looked out the balcony door windows at the mountains beyond.

His plans had been delayed. But they were far from being stopped.

# THANK YOU

I just wanted to take a moment to say thank you for reading this story.

The exciting conclusion to the the Red Ring saga of the Shadow Cell series is coming in Book 3, so I hope you'll enjoy the final piece to this exciting puzzle I've created.

After that, the Shadow Cell will be back in action to chase other threats to civilization, so be sure to stay tuned for more intense action from the ladies of Shadow Cell.

I know that you have millions of choices when it comes to reading, and I'm honored that you chose to spend some time with this story. There is no privilege greater for a writer.

So, thank you, from the bottom of my heart. I appreciate it.

Ernest

# OTHER BOOKS BY ERNEST DEMPSEY

Sean Wyatt Series:

The Secret of the Stones

The Cleric's Vault

The Last Chamber

The Grecian Manifesto

The Norse Directive

Game of Shadows

The Jerusalem Creed

The Samurai Cipher

The Cairo Vendetta

The Uluru Code

The Excalibur Key

The Denali Deception

The Sahara Legacy

The Fourth Prophecy

Adriana Villa Series:

War of Thieves Box Set

When Shadows Call (Shadow Cell Book 1)

*For Mark Dawson, James Blatch, John Dyer, and Nick Stephenson. Thanks for everything, guys.*